SEA-MEW ABBEY

SEA MEW ABBEY

FLORENCE WARDEN

Originally published in 1899.

Published by Wildside Press.
Visit us online at wildsidepress.com.

CHAPTER I.

ABOUT a quarter of a century ago, under a bright May morning sun, the English Channel Squadron steamed into the harbour of the French town of Harbourg, with flags half-mast high. The Captain of one of the vessels had lost his young wife that morning.

Until the very hour of her death, the poor fellow had persisted in believing that she was getting better, that the weakness which had been growing for months on the fragile little lady, the paleness of her delicate cheeks, the feebleness of her sweet voice would pass away. And now they had indeed passed away—into waxen death, and the twenty-year-old wife lay peacefully in the little state cabin, while her husband, stunned by uncomprehending grief, stood beside her with her baby in his arms, not hearing its soft babble of inarticulate sounds, not seeing anything but that horrible, agonising, still image of the woman he had frantically loved.

"Speak to mamma, baby, wake her, wake her!" he had cried when, noticing how still and white his wife had grown, and refusing to own the truth, he had rushed out of the cabin, snatched the child from its nurse, and held out its little warm arms towards its mother. But the white, thin arms had lost their tenderness, and lay still; the cold mouth met that of the child with no loving kiss; and as the great brown eyes stared fixedly and without meaning at the ceiling, where the reflection of the sparkling blue water outside danced and shimmered, the man's heart was torn by a pang of maddened comprehension, and a black pall was cast for ever, for him, upon the whole world.

Six hours later, when the sun was declining, and a fresh breeze was blowing from the sea, and the angelus was sounding from the chapel of the grey-walled convent, whose turrets rose up high upon the cliffs above the town, a stranger rang for admission at the convent-gate. The little sister who peeped at him through the wicket and then slowly opened the door, was rather alarmed by his appearance, and found the foreign accent in which he asked to see the Mother-Superior difficult to understand. But she would not have dared deny him admittance, for there was something in his curt tone and manner which would have made refusal of any demand of his impossible to the meek nun.

As the Gothic-pointed outer door clanged to behind them, and the stranger stepped in out of the shining sunlight into the darkness of the white-washed cloisters, a little cry rose up from the burden he carried in his arms, and the woman's heart went out in an instant to the hidden morsel of humanity.

"Holy mother!" cried she, "it's a child! Let me see it, monsieur."

The stranger's hard features did not soften, but a light came into his eyes as he drew aside the shawl which covered the child and showed a weird, pale little face, with great frightened dark eyes.

"She has no mother?" whispered the sister, with quick apprehension and sympathy.

"God help her! no,—unless," and the man's hoarse voice trembled,—"unless she finds one here."

The sound of sweet singing from the little chapel began to be heard, muffled, through the cloister walls, and then it swelled louder as the chapel door opened, and another dark-robed woman peeped out, hearing the strange footsteps and a man's voice.

"Come," said the portress briskly, "this way, monsieur, you shall see the Mother-Superior yourself."

The smell of the white lilac came in from the quiet garden as they passed through the cloister, and entered a great, square, bare-looking room, with a floor polished like glass, high white-washed walls, a round table, and a regiment of rush-bottomed chairs placed stiffly against the wainscoting. A very large plain bookcase containing brightly-bound religious and devotional works, a gloomy-looking oil-painting of a former Mother-Superior, and a black stove standing out from the wall, completed the furniture of the convent visitors' room.

After some delay, the Mother-Superior came in. She was an elderly lady with a face of intellectual type, to which the habit of her Order gave a look of some severity. The stranger took in every detail of her appearance with a searching look, and opened his business abruptly.

"I am in great trouble, madam," he began, in a harsh voice, "where to find a home for my little girl. And as I was wondering, down in the harbour there, what I should do with her, I saw your walls looking down over the water, and heard your bells, and I thought perhaps she might find a shelter here. I am a sailor, and I have—no one to trust her with."

His voice got out of his control on the last words. The Superior looked perplexed, but not yielding. As he unfolded the shawl which was wrapped round the child, she gently shook her head.

"We couldn't undertake the care of a child as young as that," she said, not unkindly. "She can't be more than two."

"That's all," said her father.

"Her mother——" began the Superior gently.

"Died this morning," said he hoarsely.

"Oh!" The lady uttered this exclamation in a low voice, and bent at once over the child, taking its little hand tenderly. "I am afraid my sombre robe may frighten her," she said.

But the child did not draw back, only looked wonderingly at the lined face, at the snowy linen and the thick black veil.

"Is she of our religion?"

"No."

"But you of course wish her to be brought up a Catholic?"

"No."

The good Mother looked up in surprise.

"Then what induced you to bring her here?"

"Where women are I expected to find kindness and mercy for my motherless child."

"You are English, monsieur?"

"Yes."

"And you would trust Catholics, Frenchwomen, as much as that?"

"I have been a traveller, madam, and I am no bigot."

The Superior, with her face wrinkled up with deepest perplexity, looked from him to the child, who had stretched out her tiny fingers for the rosary.

"You see this omen. Does not that frighten you?"

The stranger hesitated, and looked down upon his little daughter, who was clasping the crucifix with delight. Like most sailors, of high and low degree, he was superstitious.

"One must risk something," he said at last bluntly. "And if I'm ready to risk that, surely you might give way."

"I would if I could. My heart yearns to the poor little creature. But she would be very unsuitably placed here. Have you no friends, no relations, who would take charge of her?"

He laughed shortly.

"Plenty. I am not a poor man, madam; I did not use that as an inducement to you, for it's not money-bought kindness I want for my—my poor wife's child. But you could name what sum you like for her keep, education, anything."

"I had not thought of that, monsieur," said the Superior, with more dignity. "We take older girls to educate, but——"

"But not my poor lame baby. Very well."

He was wrapping the child up quickly, when the Superior stopped him by one word uttered in a different tone.

"Stop!"

The stranger, without pausing in his work, looked up.

"*Lame*, did you say?"

"Yes, I said lame," he answered shortly. "I had forgotten that further disqualification. A d——, I mean a fool of a nurse dropped her on the deck when she was seven months old, and—and she's lame, will always

3

be so. Come, Freda, we'll get out in the sunshine and warm ourselves again."

The great room was cold, and the child's lips and nails began to look blue. But before he could reach the door, he saw the black garments beside him again, and with a quick, strong, peremptory movement the child was taken out of his arms.

"Lame! Poor angel. You should have told me that before."

The heavy veil drooped over the little one, and the father knew that she had found a home.

"God bless you, and all the saints too, madam, if it comes to that!" he said with a tremor in his voice. And he cleared his throat two or three times as, with uncertain, fumbling fingers, he searched for something in his pockets.

At last he drew out a soiled envelope, which he placed upon the table. It was directed simply "To the Mother-Superior, Convent of the Sacred Heart." The lady read the direction with surprise.

"You were pretty sure of success in your mission, then, when you came up here?"

"Yes, madam, I have always believed I could succeed in everything—until—this morning."

His harsh voice broke again.

"You will find in that envelope an address from which any communication will be forwarded to me. It is an old house on the Yorkshire coast, which has been shut up now for many years. But there is a caretaker who will send on letters."

"And some day you will open the place again, and want your daughter to keep house for you?"

He shook his head.

"It's a lonely place, and would frighten a girl. The birds build their nests about it. I believe the towns-folk have named it Sea-Mew Abbey. Good-bye, madam, and thank you for your goodness. Good-bye, Freda."

He printed one hasty kiss on the pale baby face of his daughter, and the next moment his heavy footsteps were echoing down the cloister. The Mother-Superior heard the outer door clang behind him and shut him out into the world again, and then, still clasping the child in her arms, she opened the envelope which the stranger had left. It contained English bank-notes for fifty pounds, and a card with the following name and address on it:

"CAPTAIN MULGRAVE, R. N.,
"St. Edelfled's, Presterby, Yorkshire."

As she read the words, the child in her arms began to cry. At the sound of the little one's voice, one of the many doors of the room softly opened; and secure from observation, as they thought, two or three of the sombrely clad sisters peeped curiously in.

But the good Mother's eyes had grown keen with long watchfulness; she saw the white-framed faces as the door hurriedly closed.

"Sister Monica, Sister Theresa!" she called, but in no stern voice.

And the two nuns, trembling and abashed, but not sorry to be on the point of having their curiosity satisfied even at the cost of a rebuke, came softly in.

"We have a new little inmate," said the Superior in a solemn voice, "a tender young creature whom God, for His own all-wise purposes, has chastened by two severe misfortunes, even at this early age. She is lame, and she has lost her earthly mother."

A soft murmur of sympathy, low, yet so full that it seemed as if other voices from the dim background took it up and prolonged it, formed a sweet chorus to the kindly-spoken words. The Superior went on:

"I have promised the father of this child that, so far as by the help of God and His blessed saints we may, we will supply the place of the blessings she has lost. Will you help me, all of you? Yes, all of you."

And again the soft murmur "Yes, yes," of the two nuns before her was taken up by a dimly-seen chorus.

"Come in, then, and kiss your little sister."

They trooped in softly, the dark-robed nuns, their rosaries jangling on the bare boards as they knelt, one by one, and kissed the tiny soft face of the child in the Superior's arms. Bending close to the baby in the dim twilight which had now fallen on convent and garden, until the snowy linen about their calm faces fell with cold touch on the tiny hands, they scanned the childish features lovingly, and rose up one by one, bound by holy promises of tenderness and sympathy to the little one.

And so, before the evening primroses in the convent garden had shut up their pale faces for the night, and the cattle had been driven to their sheds on the hill, Freda Mulgrave was no longer motherless.

CHAPTER II.

THE years rippled away so quietly at the convent that Freda Mulgrave shot up into a slender girl of eighteen while yet the remembrance of her romantic arrival was fresh in the minds of the good sisters. During all this time her father had given no sign of interest in her existence beyond the transmission of half-yearly cheques to the Mother-Superior for her maintenance and education. When, therefore, she declared her wish to become a nun, and Captain Mulgrave's consent was asked as scarcely more than a matter of form, his reply, which came by telegraph, filled Freda and her companions with surprise.

This was the message:

> "Send my daughter to me immediately. Train to Dieppe; boat to Newhaven; train to Victoria, London; cab to King's Cross; train to Presterby.
>
> > "JOHN MULGRAVE,
> > "St. Edelfled's."

From the moment Freda read the telegram until the bitterly cold afternoon on which she found herself approaching her new Yorkshire home, the train labouring heavily through the snow, she seemed to live in a wild dream. She sat back in her corner, growing drowsy in the darkness, as the train, going more and more slowly, wound its way through a narrow, rock-bound valley, and at last entered a cutting down the sides of which the snow was slipping in huge white masses. The snorting of the two engines sounded louder, every revolution of the wheels was like a great heart-beat shivering through the whole train. Then the expected moment came, the engine stopped.

Freda heard the shouts of men as the passengers got out of the carriages, and then a rough-looking, broad-shouldered fellow climbed up to the door of her compartment, and called to her.

"Hallo! Hallo! Anybody here?" he cried, in a strange, uncouth accent. "Why, it's t' little lame lass, sewerly! Are ye all reeght?"

"Yes, thank you," answered Freda. "An accident has happened, hasn't it?"

"Ay, we're snawed oop. Wheer were ye going to, missie? To Presterby?"

"Yes. Is it far?"

"A matter o' nine mile or so."

"And you don't think we can get there to-night?"

6

"Noa. We're fast. But there's an inn nigh here, a little pleace, but better shelter nor this, an' we could get food an' foire theer. Ah'm afreed ye'll find it rough getting through t' snaw. But we must try an' manage it, or ye'll die o' cawld."

Freda hesitated.

"I suppose there's no way of letting my father know!"

"Who is your father, missie?"

"Captain Mulgrave, of St. Edelfled's, Presterby."

The words were hardly out of her mouth when, as if by magic, a great change came over her companion. The hearty, good-natured, genial manner at once left him, and he became cold, cautious and quiet.

"Rough Jock's daughter! Whew!" he whistled softly to himself.

"Rough Jock!" repeated Freda curiously. "That's not my father's name!"

"Noa, missie, but it's what some folks calls him about here; leastways, so Ah've heerd tell," he added cautiously. "Now," he continued after a pause, "Ah'll do what Ah can for ye. An' ye'll tell 'Fox'—noa, Ah mean ye'll tell Cap'n Mulgrave how ye were takken aht o' t' snaw-drift by Barnabas Ugthorpe."

"Barnabas Ugthorpe!" softly repeated Freda, marvelling at the uncouth title.

"Ay, it's not a very pretty neame, and it doan't belong to a very pretty fellow," said Barnabas, truly enough, "but to a honest," he went on emphatically, with a large aspirate; "an' me and my missis have ruled t' roast at Curley Home Farm fifteen year coom next Martinmas, an' my feyther and my grandfeyther and their feythers afore that, mebbe as long as t' family o' Captain Mulgrave has lived at Sea-Mew Abbey."

Without further parley, the stout farmer opened the door; and taking the girl up, crutch and all, as if she had been a child, carried her along the line, up a steep path on to the snow-covered moor above, and across to a lonely-looking stone-built inn, into which the passengers from the snowed-up train were straggling in twos and threes.

The accommodation at the "Barley Mow" was of the most modest sort, and the proprietor, Josiah Kemm, a big, burly Yorkshireman, with a red face, seamed and crossed in all directions by shrewd, money-grabbing puckers, was at a loss where to stow this sudden influx of visitors. He opened the door of the little smoking-room, where the half-dozen travellers already penned up there made way for the lame girl beside the fire. One of them, a sturdily built middle-aged man, whose heart went out towards the fragile little lady, jumped up and said:

"Let me get you something hot to drink, and some biscuits."

7

Freda's new acquaintance was one of those men with "honest Englishman" writ large on bluff features and sturdy figure, whom you might dislike as aggressive and blunt in manner, but whom your instinct would impel you to trust. This little convent girl had no standard of masculine manners by which to judge the stranger, whose kindness opened her heart. He seemed to her very old, though in truth he was scarcely forty; and she babbled out all the circumstances of her life and journey to him with perfect confidence, in answer to the questions which he frankly and bluntly put to her.

"Mulgrave, Mulgrave!" he repeated to himself, when she had told him her name. "Of course, I remember Captain Mulgrave was the owner of the old ruin on the cliff at Presterby, popularly called 'Sea-Mew Abbey.'"

"Yes, that's it," cried Freda, with much excitement. "That is my father. Oh, sir, what is he like? Do you know him?"

"Well, I can hardly say I know him, but I've met him. It's years ago now though; I haven't been in Yorkshire for nineteen years."

"But what was he like then?"

"He was one of the smartest-looking fellows I ever saw. But he's a good deal changed since then, so I've heard. I was only a youngster when I saw him, and he made a great impression upon me. Of course he was older than I, high up in his profession, while I hadn't even entered upon mine."

"And what is yours?" asked Freda simply.

"I have a situation under government," he answered, smiling at her ingenuousness. "The way I came to hear of the change in Captain Mulgrave," he went on, "was through a brother I have in the navy. Of course you have heard the circumstances: how Captain Mulgrave shot down four men in a mutiny——"

"What!" cried the girl in horror, "my father—*killed* four men!"

"Oh, well, you are putting it too harshly—as the authorities did. Those who know best said that if only there had been one of our periodical war-scares on, a couple of shiploads of such fellows as he shot would have been better spared than a man of the stamp of Captain Mulgrave. But the affair ruined him."

"My poor father!" whispered Freda tremulously.

"I believe you wouldn't know him for the same man. But cheer up, little woman, perhaps your coming will waken up his interest in life again. I'm sure it ought to," he added kindly.

"Oh," she said in a low voice, "that is almost too good to hope; but I will pray that it may be so."

She leant back wearily in her chair, her arms slipping down at her sides. Her friend rose and left the room, speedily returning with the landlady, an untidy, down-trodden looking woman, who shook her head at the suggestion that she should find a room for the lady upstairs.

"There's a sofy in t' kitchen wheer she can lie down if she's tired. But there's a rough lot in theer, Ah tell ye. And ye, mester, can bide here. They doan't want for company yonder."

The kitchen was a large, bare, stone-flagged room, with a wide, open fireplace and rough, greyish walls. From the centre-beam hung large pieces of bacon, tied up with string in the north-country fashion. On a bare deal table was a paraffin lamp with a smoke-blackened chimney. The only other light was that thrown by the wood-fire. Freda, therefore, could see very little of the occupants of the room. But their voices, and strong Yorkshire accent, told that they belonged to a different class from that of the travellers in the bar-parlor.

These men stood or sat in small groups talking low and eagerly. Mrs. Kemm upset Freda, rather than assisted her, on to the sofa, with a nod to her husband.

"She's a soart o' furreigner, and saft besides, by t' looks on her. She'll not mind ye."

"Ah tell tha," one of the men was saying to Kemm, "Rough Jock's not a mon to play tricks with, either; tha mun be squeer wi' him, or leave him aloan. Ah' it's ma belief he wouldn't ha' quarrelled wi' t' Heritages, if t' young chaps hadn't thowt they could best him. An' see wheer they'll be if he dew break off wi' 'em! It'll be a bad deay for them if he dew!"

"Ah tell tha," said Kemm, doggedly, "he has broke off wi' 'em. As for them chaps, they weren't smart enough to do wi' a mon loike Rough Jock. That's wheer t' mischief lay. They shouldn't nivver ha' tuk on wi' him."

"Ah'm thinking if they hadn't tuk on wi' him, they'd ha' tuk on wi' t' workhouse; and that's what it'll coom to neow, if Rough Jock leaves 'em in t' lurch, wi' their proide and their empty larder! An' thur'll be wigs on t' green tew, for Bob Heritage is a nasty fellow when his blood's oop. Have a care, Josiah, have a care!"

"Oh, ay, Ah'm not afraid o' Bob Heritage, nor o' Rough Jock either; an' me an' him are loike to coom to an unnerstanding."

"Weel, ye mun knaw yer own business, Kemm; but Ah wouldn't tak' oop wi him mysen," said the third man, who had scarcely spoken.

"Not till ye gotten t' chance, eh, lad?" said Josiah stolidly. "Coom an' have a soop o' ale; it shall cost ye nowt."

He led the way out of the room; and the rest, not all at once, but by twos and threes and very quietly, followed him, until Freda was left quite alone. As she leaned upon her elbow, trying to piece together the fragments she had understood of the talk, she heard in the passage, to her great relief, a voice she recognised. It was that of her farmer friend, Barnabas Ugthorpe, who looked in at the kitchen door the next moment.

"Weel, lass," he said, cheerily, "How are ye gettin on? T' night's cleared a bit, an' Ah can tak' ye on to Owd Castle Farm. T' fowks theer are very thick wi' Capt'n Mulgrave. It isn't more'n a moile from here."

Within ten minutes a cart was at the door, and they were on their way. The road lying over a smooth expanse of moorland, and the moon giving a little more light; it was not long before a very curious building came in sight, on rising ground a little to the east of the road as it went northwards.

The front of the house, which faced south, was long and singularly irregular. At each end were the still solid-looking remains of a round tower built of great blocks of rough-hewn stone, roofed in with red tiles. Both were lighted by narrow, barred windows. Between the towers ran an outer wall of the same grey stone, much notched and ivy-grown at the top, and broken through here and there lower down to receive small square latticed windows greatly out of character with the structure. Into a breach in this wall a very plain farm-house building had been inserted, with rough white-washed surface and stone-flagged roof.

Barnabas got down, raised the knocker and gave three sounding raps.

In a few moments Freda heard rapid steps inside, and a woman's voice, harsh and strident, saying in a whisper:

"That's not the Captain, surely!"

Freda turned quickly to her companion.

"Who are these people? What is their name?"

"Their neame's Heritage," said Barnabas.

Freda started. It was the name she had heard at the "Barley Mow" as that of the family who had quarrelled with "Rough Jock."

CHAPTER III.

FREDA watched the opening of the farmhouse door with dread, as there peeped out a man's face, pale, flat, puffy, with light eyes and colourless light eyelashes. Freda took an instantaneous dislike to him, and tried to draw her companion back by the sleeve.

"What do you want at this time of night?" asked, the man pompously.

And Freda knew, by his speech and manner, that he was a man-servant, and that he was not a Yorkshireman. He now opened the door wider, and she saw that he was dressed in very shabby livery, that he was short and stout, and that a lady was standing in the narrow entrance-hall behind him. Barnabas caught sight of her too, and he hailed her without ceremony.

"Hey theer, missus," he cried cheerily, "can Ah have a word with 'ee?"

Rather under than above the middle height, dressed plainly in a black silk gown, Mrs. Heritage was a woman who had been very pretty, and who would have been so still but for a certain discontented, worried look, which seemed to have eaten untimely furrows into her handsome features.

"Well, Mr. Ugthorpe, and what do you want?"

"Here's a young gentlewoman without a shelter for her head, an' Ah thowt ye would be t' person to give it her."

"Young gentlewoman—without shelter!" echoed the lady in slow, solemn, strident tones. "Why, how's that?"

"I was snowed up in the train, madam, on my way to my father's. And we are very sorry to have troubled you. Good-night."

Very proudly the girl uttered these last words, in the high, tremulous tones that tell of tears not far off. While Barnabas stopped at the door to argue and explain, Freda was hopping back through the snow towards the lane as fast as she could, with bitter mortification in her heart, and a weary numbness creeping through her limbs.

Suddenly through the night air there rang a cry in a deep, full, man's voice, a voice that thrilled Freda to the heart, calling to something within her, stirring her blood.

"Aunt, she's lame! Don't you see she's lame?"

She heard rapid footsteps in the snow. As she turned to see who it was that was pursuing her, and at the same time raised her hand to dash away the rising tears and clear her sight, her little crutch fell. She stooped to grope in the snow, and instantly felt a pair of strong arms around her. Not Barnabas Ugthorpe's. There was no impetuous acting upon impulse about Barnabas. And in the pressure of these unknown arms there seemed to Freda to be a kindly, protecting warmth and comfort such as she had never felt before.

"Who is it? Who are you?" she cried tremulously.

"Never mind, I've been sent to take care of you," answered the voice.

Again it thrilled Freda; and she was silent, rather frightened. She gave one feeble struggle, seeing nothing through her tears in the darkness, and her ungloved hand touched a man's moustache. To the convent-bred girl this seemed a shocking accident: she was dumb from that moment with shame and confusion. The good-humoured remonstrance of the unseen one caused her the keenest anguish.

"Oh, you ungrateful little thing. You've scratched my face most horribly, and I don't believe there's a bit of sticking-plaster in the house. Next time I shall leave you to sleep in the snow."

"I—I am sorry. I beg your pardon," she faltered. "I did not see."

"All right. I'll forgive you this once. Not that I think you've apologised half enough."

At first she took this as a serious reproach, and wondered what she could say to soothe his wounded feelings. But the next moment, being quick-witted, she began dimly to understand that she was being laughed at, and she resolved to hold her peace until she could see the face of this creature, who was evidently of a kind quite new to her experience, with puzzling manners and a way of looking at things which was not that of the nuns of the Sacred Heart.

In a few moments Freda heard the voice of Barnabas thanking Mrs. Heritage for her good cheer as he came out of the house. Then she found herself put gently down on her feet inside the doorway, while she heard the strident tones of the lady of the house, asking her not unkindly whether she was wet and cold. But even her kindness grated on Freda; it was hard, perfunctory, she thought. There was all the time, behind the thoughtful hospitality for her unexpected guest, some black care sitting, engrossing the best of her. Mrs. Heritage hurried on, through a labyrinth of rooms and passages, to an oaken door, old and worm-eaten, studded with rusty nails.

"This room," she said, turning back as the door rolled slowly inwards, "is the one wreck of decent life on which we pride ourselves. It is the old banqueting-hall of the castle. We took it into use, after an hundred and fifty years' neglect, when we were obliged to come and bury ourselves here."

It was a long and lofty room with a roof of oak so ancient that many of the beams were eaten away by age. The walls were of rough stone, hung, to a height of six feet from the ground, with worn tapestry, neatly patched and mended. The hall was lighted by six Gothic windows on each side, all of them ten feet from the ground. The furniture, of shabby and worm-eaten oak, consisted chiefly of a number of presses and settles, quaintly shaped and heavy-looking, which lined the walls. On one end of a long table in the middle, supper was spread, while at the further end of the hall a log-fire burned in a large open fireplace.

"Where is Richard?" asked Mrs. Heritage solemnly, just as the door was pushed open, and three or four dogs bounded in, followed by a tall young man in knickerbockers and a Norfolk jacket, with a dog-whip sticking out of his pocket. It was Freda's unknown friend.

"Let me introduce you," said his aunt. "My nephew, Mr. Richard Heritage to—— What is your name, child?"

Freda hesitated. Then, with the blood surging in her head, she answered in a clear voice:

"Freda Mulgrave."

She had expected to give them a surprise; but she had not reckoned upon giving such a shock to Mrs. Heritage as the announcement plainly caused her. Dick, whose careless glance had, for some reason which she did not understand, pained her, at once turned to her with interest.

"You know my father. What is he like?" she ventured presently, in a timid voice, to Mrs. Heritage, when she had explained how she came to be travelling alone to Presterby.

"He is a tall, dignified-looking gentleman, my dear, with a silver-grey beard and handsome eyes."

"And does he live all by himself?"

"I believe his establishment consists of a housekeeper, and her husband, who was one of his crew."

"And decidedly a rough-looking customer, as you will say when you see him, Miss Mulgrave," chimed in Dick. "This Crispin Bean, who belonged to Captain Mulgrave's ship at the time of the—the little difficulty which ended in his withdrawing from the Navy, has followed him like a dog ever since. It's no ordinary man who can inspire such enthusiasm as that," he went on, as he stood by the big fireplace, and kicked one of the burning logs into a fresh blaze. "You must have noticed," he said presently, "that the discovery of your being your father's daughter had some special interest for us?"

"Yes, I did think so," said Freda.

"You see," Dick went on, pulling his moustache and twisting up the ends ferociously, "we're very poor, poor as rats. It's Free Trade has done it. We—my cousin and I—have to farm our own land; and as we can't afford the railway rates, we sell what we produce to our neighbours. If they left off buying we couldn't live. Well, my cousin and your father have had a quarrel, and we're afraid Captain Mulgrave won't buy of us any more. You understand, don't you?"

"Oh, yes," said Freda slowly, struggling with her sleepy senses. "He has quarrelled with your cousin, and so you're afraid he'll buy what he wants not from you but from Josiah Kemm."

Both her hearers started violently, and Freda perceived that she had let out something he had not known.

"I stayed for an hour at an inn called the 'Barley Mow,'" she explained, "and I heard something there which I think must have had some meaning like that. But perhaps I am wrong. I am tired, confused—I——"

Her voice grew faint and drowsy. Dick glanced at Mrs. Heritage.

"Don't trouble your head about it to-night," said he. "You are tired. Aunt, take Miss Mulgrave to her room. Good-night."

And poor Freda, sleepy, contrite, was hurried off to bed.

Next morning she was down early, but she saw nothing of Dick. The mistress of the house read prayers in a tone of command rather than of supplication; and, as the servants filed out afterwards, she called the butler, and asked:

"What is this I hear about Master Richard's going off on 'Roan Mary' at this time in the morning?"

"It's a telegram he wants to send to Master Robert; and he has to ride to Pickering because the snow's broken down the wires on this side," answered Blewitt sullenly. "I saw the message. It said: 'He is on with Kemm. Call on your way back.'"

Freda caught the name "Kemm." She felt very uncomfortable, but nobody noticed her, and she was suddenly startled by an outbreak of sobs and moans from Mrs. Heritage, who had begun to pace up and down the room.

"That'll do," said Blewitt sullenly, "I'm going to have a talk with you, ma'am. We'd best have things square before your precious son Robert comes back. I want to know when I'm to have my wages. I don't mean my thirty-five pounds a year for waiting at table, but the wages I was promised for more important work."

"I will speak to Mr. Robert as soon as he returns, Blewitt," said Mrs. Heritage, who was evidently in a paroxysm of terror. "I am quite sure——"

"That I shall get no good out of *him*," went on Blewitt, doggedly. "Do you think I don't know Mr. Robert? Why, miss," and the man turned, with a sudden change of manner to deprecating respect, to Freda, "your father, Captain Mulgrave, knows what Mr. Robert is, and that's why he's made up his mind, like the wise gentleman he is, not to have anything more to do with him. And *I've* made up *my* mind," he went on with vicious emphasis, heeding neither Mrs. Heritage's spasmodic attempts to silence him, nor the young girl's timid remonstrances, "either to have my due or to follow his example."

Freda had crept up, with her little crutch, to Mrs. Heritage's side, and was offering the mute comfort of a sympathetic hand thrust into that of the lady.

"Run away, my dear child, run away," whispered the latter eagerly.

The man went on in a brutal tone:

"I'm not such a fool as Master Dick, to stay here and be made a catspaw of, while your precious son goes off to enjoy himself. Why should some do all the work, and others——"

The rest of his sentence was lost to Freda, who had got outside the door into a great bare apartment beyond. Here, lifting the latch of a little modern door which most inappropriately filled an old Gothic doorway, she found herself, as she had expected, in the courtyard.

CHAPTER IV.

FREDA crossed the courtyard to one of the ruined corner-towers, and finding the staircase still practicable, continued her wanderings, with cautious steps, along the top of the broken castle-wall. She got along easily as far as the thatched roof of a big barn. But here her crutch slipped on the snow and went crashing through a tarpaulin-covered hole in the thatch, carrying its owner with it, into a loft half-filled with hay. There was no way of escape until somebody came by to rescue her. Freda therefore could do nothing but look down into the hazy light of the barn below; and presently, nursed into a comfortable warmth by the hay, she fell asleep.

She was awakened by being shaken pretty roughly, while a voice cried close to her ear:

"Now, then, I've got you; and if I let you get home with a whole bone in your little thievish body, you may think yourself jolly lucky, I can tell you."

Having recognised the voice as Dick's, Freda was not alarmed by the assumed ferocity of his tone. Besides, he had evidently mistaken her for somebody else. So she shook herself free from the hay, and sat up and looked at him. By that time he had got used to the gloom of the loft, and to her surprise, he drew back so quickly that he risked falling off the ladder. A little more contemplation, and then he murmured:

"Of course—it's the hair!"

The net in which, in primitive fashion, she was accustomed to tuck away her hair, had been lost in her tumble through the roof, and her red-brown locks, which had a pretty, natural wave, had fallen about her ears and given to her pale face quite a new character. Dick, however, was not a young fellow looking idly at a pretty girl, but a man full of responsibilities and anxieties.

"You said last night," he began abruptly, "that you had heard something at the 'Barley Mow' about us and your father. What was it?"

She answered in a low, modest voice, but without any fear.

"You say my father is quarrelling with you. You wish to find out all his movements. Then if I tell you about them, I am betraying my own father!"

"I warn you that your principles won't agree with his any more than they do with mine. Do as you *would be* done by is what you were taught at the convent, I suppose. Do as you *are* done by is the motto we live by here."

"It seems very dreadful," whispered Freda, "to do things that are wrong and not to mind!"

And the young man perceived that she had tears in her eyes.

16

"Don't cry," said he gently. "I shouldn't have said what I have to you but that I wanted you to go back to your convent before you hear anything more to pain you. I want to take you to Presterby this afternoon, without your seeing my cousin Bob."

"Ah!" cried Freda with a start. "Your cousin! Tell me, is he good to you? Are you fond of him?"

"Not particularly. That answer will do to both questions."

"Then why do you stay here? Would it not be better for you to go away? They say—do they not say, that he makes you work for his advantage?"

He paused a few moments, and his face grew graver. Then he said abruptly: "Supposing I were to tell you that I am content to be taken advantage of, and that I'd rather live on here anyhow than like a prince anywhere else. I tell you," he went on, with the ring of passion in his voice, "I love every foot of ground about here as you love your convent and your nuns; the stones of this old place are my religion. And so I shall live on here in some sort of hole-and-corner fashion, bringing grist to a mill that gives me neither honour nor profit, until——"

He stopped short. Freda was deeply moved; but she only asked him, in a constrained voice, if he would let her come down the ladder. He ran rapidly down, held the ladder firm for her, and gently assisted her as she came near the ground, taking her crutch and returning it to her when her feet touched the floor.

"Poor little lame girl!" said he softly, and the words brought sobs into her throat. "Why, you're crying! I didn't hurt you, did I?"

"No-o, no," said Freda, drawing herself away. "Let me go, please."

"Well, say that we're friends first."

Freda raised her eyes, but her glance passed Dick and remained fixed on a face that appeared at the window beyond. A young man, with sandy hair and moustache, was looking in with a cynical grin. Dick turned quickly, when he saw the change on the girl's face. His own expression altered also.

"Bob! Back already!" he cried.

The young man had climbed in. Nodding at his cousin, with a glance at Freda which she found exceedingly offensive, he asked:

"Well, and who is the little girl?"

Perhaps the girl's mind, having retained a child-like purity, was able at once to detect the taint in that of Robert Heritage; but certainly the persistent stare of his small grey eyes, which he honestly believed to be irresistible, affected her no more than the gleam of a couple of marbles; while every other feature of his face, from the obtrusively pointed nose to the thin-lipped mouth, seemed to her to betray ugly qualities, the names of which she scarcely knew. He, on his side, regarded her face with a bold, critical stare, which changed into contempt the moment he caught sight of her crutch. Dick grew red with anger.

"You didn't get my telegram then?" he said shortly, interposing his person to shield the girl from his cousin's impudent gaze.

"No, I got no telegram. What was it about?"

"Come into the house and I'll tell you."

He moved to the door. Robert would not let him open it.

"What! and interrupt your studies of the maim, the halt, and the blind?" he asked, in a low voice which, however, the girl's quick ears caught.

Freda had been reprimanded at the convent for occasional outbursts of passion. But she had never yet felt the force of such a torrent of indignation as seemed to sweep through her frame at this, the first sneer at her infirmity she had ever heard. She scarcely noticed Dick's angry remonstrance; but raising her flushed face to Robert, she said:

"You can sneer at me now. Perhaps you will not when I am in the house of my father, Captain Mulgrave."

"Come, that's rather strong, little girl," he said coolly. "To be Mulgrave's daughter—which you may be for anything I know—is one thing, but to live in his house is another. I can assure you he has made no preparations for your reception."

His insolent tone stung Freda to a greater heat of passion.

"Perhaps you are not in my father's confidence," she said in a voice which shook a little. "If you had been, you might have known that he was going to visit Josiah Kemm."

Without waiting to see the effect of her words, Freda ran out of the barn, across the court-yard, and up to the room she had slept in. There she put on her hat and cloak, and after waiting some time in fear lest she might be hunted out, stole out of the room and came, to her disgust, face to face with Blewitt. He had on a thick coat and riding-boots.

"I beg pardon, ma'am, but I was a-coming to inform you that I have been hordered by Mr. 'Eritage to go to the Abbey with a letter for your respected father, Captain Mulgrave. Now, ma'am, I should esteem it a honour to be sent to a gentleman like Captain Mulgrave on any hordinary errand. But knowing, as I happen to do, the himport of the letter, I feel it very different, I assure you, ma'am."

Freda was too unsophisticated to guess by what simple means Blewitt had arrived at the knowledge he alluded to. But she was afraid he wanted to tell her something she ought not to hear, and she interrupted him hurriedly.

"Yes, I'm sure that all you say is quite—quite right," she said nervously. "But I—I am going out, and I cannot——"

"You cannot stay under the roof of such people as them. Which I was sure, ma'am, that such would be your feelings. Barnabas Ugthorpe, the farmer, has been here with his cart a-inquiring after you; and I know where he is to be found now, if so be as you would like me to show you how to get out by a private door."

"Oh, yes, please show me out," cried Freda piteously, delighted at the thought of seeing her rough friend, whom she hoped to persuade to take her on to the Abbey.

"I will do so, ma'am," answered Blewitt, who by this promise forced her to listen to him. "And if you could say a good word to the Captain for me that would induce him for to take a hard-working man into his service, why, I could tell him a many little tales about the goings on in this house which would astonish him, and just show him how he misplaced his confidence in some people I could name."

"How can you think my father could listen to such things!" Freda broke out indignantly.

"Well, ma'am, gentlemen's ways is not always straight ways, when they wants pertic'ler to know things," said Blewitt, drily though respectfully. "But the Captain's a 'asty and 'aughty sort of gentleman as you don't always quite know where to have him! and when he gets this letter, which threatens to do for him if he don't give up all dealings with Josiah Kemm immediate, why he'll be in such a taking that he'll be more likely to do for me than to listen to anything what I can say."

"Why do you take the letter then?"

The fact was that Mr. Blewitt did not wish to be off with the old love until he was quite sure of being on with the new. He put this to Freda, however, in a nobler light.

"You see, ma'am," said he, "so long as I take Mr. 'Eritage's wages, I must carry out his horders."

"Yes, of course, of course," said Freda, with almost a shriek of delight as Blewitt opened a little side-door and she found herself out of the house, standing in the snow under the grey old outer wall.

She found Barnabas just driving off from one of a group of cottages at the bottom of the lane. At her cry he stopped, waiting for her to come up.

"Barnabas!" she cried, quivering with anxiety, "won't you drive me over to the Abbey? Oh, do, do! You will, won't you?"

The farmer scratched his ear.

"Happen one o' t' young gentlemen 'll droive ye over."

"Oh no," said Freda quickly. "I wouldn't go back there for anything in the world!"

The farmer grinned, nodded, helped Freda into his cart, and started off at a much better pace than they had made with Josiah Kemm's old mare the night before.

"Weel, lassie," he said, as they jogged along, "ye've made a better conquest nor any scapegrace of a Heritage. That theer swell that was so kind to ye at t' 'Barley Mow,' he's gone clear creazed about ye. When Ah left ye at t' farm last neght, Ah fahnd him on t' road, mahnding for to get to Presterby. Ah towd him he couldn't the neght, an' Ah tuck him back; an' t' missus, when she'd satisfied herself he warn't a woman in disguise, was moighty civil. An' he said sooch things abaht yer having a sweet little feace, an' he said he should call at t' Abbey to see ye."

"Barnabas," said Freda suddenly, "why did you look so mysterious last night when I told you that he had something to do with the government?"

The farmer gave her an alarmed glance, as he had done the night before, and said in a cautious tone:

"Ye've gotten a pair of sharp ears, an' they hear more'n there's ony need. Ye didn't reeghtly unnerstand, lass."

After this there came a long pause, during which Freda puzzled herself as to what the inhabitants of this district had been doing, to have such a fear of the government. It was getting dark when Barnabas broke the long silence by saying, as he pointed with his whip to the summit of a hill they were about to ascend:

"T' Abbey's oop top o' theer."

Freda was too much agitated to answer except by a long-drawn breath. The Abbey! Her father's home! A terrible presentiment, natural enough after the scant experience she had had of his care, told her that there was no welcome waiting. She crouched down in the cart and clung to the farmer's arm.

"Barnabas," she whispered, "I'm afraid to go on. Drive slowly; oh, do drive slowly!"

But the robust farmer only laughed and jogged on at the same pace. The road, however, grew in a few minutes so steep that they could only proceed very slowly, and Barnabas got down to lead the horse and lighten his burden as he ploughed his way up. Traffic between the little town of Presterby and its neighbours had been so much hindered by the blockade of snow, that there were no wheel-marks on the white mass before them.

"Soomun's been riding oop a horseback, though," said Barnabas, as he looked at the print of hoofs.

"Perhaps the man Blewitt from the farm," suggested Freda. "He said he was going to ride to the Abbey."

"Oh, ay," said the farmer with interest. "If he was cooming, noa doubt it's him. Hey," he went on, in a different tone, "Ah think Ah hear his voice oop top theer! He's fell aht wi' soomun by t' sounds, Ah fancy."

He stopped the cart a moment to listen. Plainly both Freda and he could hear the voices of men in angry discussion, the one coarse and loud, the other lower and less distinguishable.

"My father!" cried Freda, trembling.

"A' reeght, lass, a' reeght; doan't ye be afraid. We'll be oop wi 'em in a breace o' sheakes."

"Barnabas! Make haste, make haste! They're quarrelling, fighting perhaps!" cried the girl in passionate excitement.

"Weel, Ah'll go and see," answered the farmer who, knowing more than his little companion did of the reckless and violent character of the disputants, was in truth as much excited as she was.

"He's carrying a letter which he said would enrage my father!" cried Freda in a tremulous voice to Barnabas, who was already some paces ahead, running up the hill as fast as he could.

The road lay between stone walls of fair height, and was full of curves and windings; so that it would have been impossible, even in broad daylight, for the farmer to see the two men until he was close upon them. He was not yet out of Freda's sight when a sharp report, followed by a second, and then by a hoarse cry, broke upon their ears. There was silence for a moment, and then the sound of galloping hoofs upon the snow. A riderless horse, bearing a man's saddle, came down the hill, with nostrils dilated and frightened eyes. Barnabas, who considered a horse as rather more a fellow-creature than a man, set to work to stop the animal before making his way to the human beings. This accomplished, he tied the horse to the gate of a field a few yards higher up, and quickening his pace again, reached the top of the hill.

Here, in the middle of the road, were two figures, the one prone on the ground, the other kneeling in the snow beside him.

The kneeling man started and rose to his feet as Barnabas came up. He held in his left hand an open letter, and in his right a revolver, which, without resistance, he allowed the farmer to take.

"Captain Mulgrave!"

The Captain only nodded. Barnabas went down in the snow beside the second figure. He was on his face, but Barnabas knew, even before he attempted to raise him, that it was Blewitt, the servant from Oldcastle Farm.

He was dead.

CHAPTER V.

THE unfortunate Blewitt had never, in his lifetime, excited the liking or respect of any one. Selfish and mean, he had been tolerated because he was useful to his employers, who mistrusted him, and feared and avoided by the rest of his neighbours. But these facts, so it seemed to Barnabas Ugthorpe, heightened the tragedy of the man-servant's death. The honest farmer could not have expressed his thought in words, he but felt that the poor wretch whose body lay at his feet had somehow lost his chance forever.

As Barnabas stood there, considering the sight before him, Captain Mulgrave, who had not uttered a word, turned quickly, and was about to climb over the stone wall to the right, on his way back to the Abbey, when he felt a strong hand on his shoulder.

"Not quite so fast, Capt'n," said Barnabas drily, "Ah want yer opinion o' this metter."

"My opinion is," said Captain Mulgrave, shortly, "that this is the most d—d mysterious thing I ever saw. And I've seen a few queer things in my life too."

"Aye," said Barnabas, "it's a bad job this."

He continued to stare at the dead man, and never once raised his eyes to the face of his living companion.

"Well," said the Captain, after a long silence, "you don't ask me to tell you how I found him?"

"Noa, sir, Ah doan't," said Barnabas drily.

"Well, why not?"

"Weel," said the farmer, scratching his ear, "Ah doan't knaw as Ah should knaw so mooch more'n Ah did afore."

"You wouldn't take my word then?"

"Ah doan't know as, oonder t' circumstances, Ah'd tek t' word o' any gentleman."

"You think I had a hand in this man's death?"

Barnabas paused a long time, still looking at the body, still scratching his ear.

"Aye, sir, it dew look like it," he admitted at last.

"Well, at first sight it, dew," mimicked Captain Mulgrave in a lighter tone than the farmer thought becoming. "But I tell you it's all d—d nonsense, I was coming down here to see what state the roads were in, and I heard men's voices, and then two shots. I was half-way across that field. I ran, got over the wall, and found the fellow lying like this, with the revolver in his hand. I took it up, and found that two chambers had been discharged. I looked up and down the lane, but I couldn't see any one."

"Noa," said Barnabas with a movement of the head, "Ah should suppose not."

He bent down over the body again, examining it.

"He's shot in t' back. Did it hissen, most loike."

"Now what reason have you for supposing I shot him?"

"Weel, sir, asking yer pardon, but to begin with, ye've gotten t' name o' being free wi' them things." And he raised the revolver, which he still held in his hand. "Then, sir, Ah happen to knaw as he came to bring ye a letter as were not loike to put ye into a good humour."

He glanced at the letter which Captain Mulgrave held.

"I don't know how you came to hear about this letter, but you're quite right as far as that is concerned. Only the man did not give it me; I found it on his dead body."

"Ye found it moighty quick then, Capt'n. That's not t' weay moast on us cooms nigh a dead mon, to begin rummaging in 's pockets before he's cawld."

"As to that, I guessed he'd come on an errand to me and had some message about him. And why should I have more respect for the fellow dead than I had for him alive? His carcase has no more value in my eyes than that of a carrion crow."

"It'll have a deal more, though, in t' eyes of a jury, Capt'n."

"Do you mean to try to hang me then, honest Barnabas?"

"Ah mean to tell what Ah seen, an' leave it to joodge an' jury to seay what they thinks on it."

"And knowing me for such a desperate character you dare to tell me this to my face?"

"Happen Ah shouldn't be so bold, but Ah gotten t' revolver mysen."

And Barnabas glanced at the weapon in his hand.

Captain Mulgrave laughed a little, and both men stood silent considering.

"I can't think who can have had such a grudge against the poor devil as to shoot him," he said at last, as if to himself. "It must have been some one on foot, for there are no hoof-marks about but those of the horse he was riding."

Barnabas said nothing. With one steady look at Captain Mulgrave as if to tell him that he hadn't done with him yet, the farmer examined the footprints in the snow round about. There were marks neither of wheels nor of hoofs further than this point, but there were footprints both of men and children, for this was the high road between Presterby and Eastborough, the next important town southwards along the coast.

"Aye," said the farmer, when he had finished his inspection, "it mun ha' been some one afoot, Capt'n, as you say."

Captain Mulgrave had been considering the aspect of the affair, and he looked more serious when Barnabas uttered these words.

"Barnabas," he said at last, "I begin to see that these devils, with their confirmed prejudice against me, may make this a serious business."

"Aye, so Ah'm thinking too."

"Give a dog a bad name, you know. Because I shot down four rascals in self-defence, I'm considered capable of depopulating the county in cold blood."

"Aye, that be so. Leastweays we knaw ye doan't hawd human loife seacred."

"Well, and that's true enough,—I don't. There are men whom I should consider it justifiable to exterminate like vermin."

"Weel, sir, we moast on us thinks that in our seacret hearts, only we moightn't knaw wheer to stop if we let ourselves begin. But when we foind a mon wi' t' courage o' these opinions, we have to put a stop to his little games pretty quick. It's not that Ah bear ye any ill-will, Capt'n, quoite t' contrary: ye have t' sympathy of all t' coontry-soide, as ye knaw. But we must draw t' loine soomwheer, an' Ah draw it at murder."

"You won't take my word?"

"Can't, Capt'n."

"Will you take my money?"

"Noa, sir."

"What are you going to do then? Go down into the town and set the police after me?"

Barnabas looked for a few moments puzzled and distressed. He would have given this high-handed gentleman into custody without a moment's hesitation if it had not been for his little daughter, now on her way to her unknown home all unconscious of the tragedy which darkened it. On the other hand, he shrank from giving her into the care of a man whose hands were reeking with the guilt of a most cowardly murder. After pondering the matter, an idea struck him, and he raised his head with a clear countenance.

"Ah'll haud my toongue aboot this business, if so be ye're ready to mak' a bargain."

"Name your price then."

"My price is that ye'll give us yer room in these parts instead of yer coompany. Ye've gotten a yacht, Capt'n, an' a rich mon's weays o' gettin' aboot an' makhin' yerself comfortable. So Ah'm not droiving a hard bargain. But ye mun be aht of t' Abbey by to-morrow, an' all ye gotten to do is to mak' soom provision for your little darter."

Captain Mulgrave was more startled by the three last words than by all the rest of the farmer's speech.

"My little daughter!" he repeated in a scoffing tone. "Yes, I'd forgotten her. But what do you know about her, eh?"

"Ah was bringing her oop t' Abbey," answered Barnabas, jerking his head and his thumb in the direction of the cart, which, however, was not in sight.

Captain Mulgrave frowned.

"D——d nuisance!" he muttered to himself.

"Eh, but Ah think Ah'll tak' her aweay again till ye're gone, Capt'n," said Barnabas drily. "T' owd stoans will give her a better welcome home than ye seem loike to."

"No, you may as well take her up now. I shall not see her. You don't want to keep the girl out all day in the cold. I'll just get across to the house now and tell Mrs. Bean to make a fire for her. By the time the cart comes round to the front I—I——" He hesitated, and Barnabas saw that, under his devil-may-care manner, Captain Mulgrave was agitated. "By that time," continued he, recovering himself, "it will be all ready for her, and—she'll see nothing of me—I shall go away—to-night—I shall be glad to. I'm sick of this pestilential country, where one can only breathe by virtue of a special act of parliament. Sha'n't see you again, Barnabas." He moved away, and just as he put his hand on the stone wall to vault over, he turned his head to say, "Thanks for your kindness to the little one."

Then he disappeared from the farmer's sight hastily, as he heard the cart groaning and squeaking up the hill.

Freda had got tired of waiting for Barnabas, and after much vigorous shaking of the reins, which he had put into her hands, she had succeeded in starting the horse again.

"Barnabas!" she cried, as soon as she caught sight, in the gloom, of the farmer's figure, "is that you?"

"Aye, lassie," said he, placing himself between the cart and the dead body on the ground.

"Didn't I hear you talking?"

"Aye, happen ye did."

"Who were you talking to?"

"Eh, lass?" said he, pretending not to hear her, so that he might gain time for reflection.

"Who—were—you—talking to?" she asked slowly but querulously, for she was cold and tired, and full of misgivings.

"Eh, but Ah was talking to a mon as were passing."

"Passing? He didn't pass me."

"Noa, lass, Ah didn't seay as he did. Ye're mighty sharp."

"It's because I don't understand you. There's something different about your manners. Something's happened, I believe!"

25

"Eh, lassie, why, what's coom over ye?"

"What's that on the ground?"

She almost shrieked this, guessing something.

"Ye've gotten too sharp eyes, lassie. Ye'd better not ask questions."

"Barnabas, Oh!—Barnabas, it's not—not—my father!" whispered the poor child, clinging, over the side of the cart, to the rough hands the farmer held out to her.

"Noa, lass, noa."

"Who is it? Tell me, quick."

"Why, lass, it's a poor mon as—as has been hurt."

"He's dead. He wouldn't be there, so still, like that, if he was not—dead," she whispered. "Who is it? Tell me, Barnabas."

"Weel, Ah have a noetion—that he's soommet loike servant Blewitt, oop to Owdcastle Farm."

"Oh, Barnabas, it's dreadful! Is he really dead?"

But she wanted no answer. She put her hands before her face, reproaching herself for having disliked the man, almost feeling that she had had a share in his tragic death.

"Who did it?" she asked at last, very suddenly.

Now Barnabas meant most strongly that the girl should not have the least suspicion that her father had a hand in this affair. The farmer's soft heart had been touched as soon as Captain Mulgrave betrayed, by a momentary breaking of the voice, that he was not so utterly indifferent to his daughter as he wished to appear. Upon that reassuring sign of human feeling, Barnabas instantly resolved to hold his tongue for ever as to what he had seen. But unluckily, his powers of imagination and dissimulation were not great. Feminine wits saw through him, as they had done many a time before. While he was slowly preparing an elaborate answer, Freda had jumped at once to the very conclusion he wished her to avoid.

"Who did it?" she repeated in tones so suddenly tremulous and passionate that they betrayed her thought even to the somewhat slow-witted Yorkshireman.

"Lord have mercy on t' lass!" cried he below his breath. "But Ah believe she knows."

"Do you mean to say," she went on in a low, monotonous voice, "that you *saw* my father—kill him?"

Her voice dropped on the last words so that Barnabas could only guess them.

"Noa, lass, noa," said he quickly, "Ah didn't *see* him do it."

"Then he didn't do it!" cried she, with a sudden change to a high key, and in tones of triumphant conviction. "You can tell me all about it now, for I'm quite satisfied."

26

"It's more'n Ah be, though," said he dubiously. "Ah found him standing over t' corpse loike this 'ere, wi' this in his hand." He produced the revolver from his pocket. "And in t' other hand he gotten letter ye spoake of, lass, that ye said would enreage him."

"And what did he say? Did you accuse him?"

"He said he didn't do it, an' Ah, why, Ah didn't believe him."

"But I do," said Freda calmly.

"Weel, but who could ha' done it then?" asked he, hoping that she might have a reason to give which would bring satisfaction to his mind also.

But in Freda's education faith and authority had been put before reason, and her answer was not one which could carry conviction to a masculine understanding.

"My father," she said solemnly, "could not commit a murder."

"Weel, soom folks' feythers does, why not your feyther? There was nobody else to do it, an' t' poor feller couldn't ha' done it hissen, for he was shot in t' back."

"I will never believe my father did it," said Freda.

"Happen he'll tell ye he did."

Freda shook her head.

"I have been very foolish," she said at last, "to listen to all the things I have heard said against him. And perhaps it is as a punishment to me that I have heard this. He was good and kind when I was a baby: how can he be bad now? And if he has done bad things since then, the Holy Spirit will come down into his heart again now, if I pray for him."

"Amen," said Barnabas solemnly.

This farmer had no more definite religion himself than that there was a Great Being somewhere, a long way off behind the clouds, whom it was no use railing at, though he didn't encourage honest industry as much as he might, and whom it was the parson's duty to keep in good humour by baptisms, and sermons, and ringing of the church-bells. But he had, nevertheless, a belief in the more lively religion of women, and thought—always in a vague way—that it brought good luck upon the world. So he took off his hat reverently when the girl was giving utterance to her simple belief, and then he led the horse past the dead body, and jumping up into the cart beside her, took up the reins.

CHAPTER VI.

AFTER a little more jolting along the highroad they turned to the right up one less used, and soon came in full sight of the Abbey ruins. Just a jagged dark grey mass they looked by the murky light of this dull evening, with here and there a jutting point upwards, the outline of the broken walls softened by the snow.

Freda sat quite silent, awestruck by the circumstances of her arrival, and by the wild loneliness of the place. A little further, and they could see the grey sea and the high cliffs frowning above it. Barnabas glanced down at the grave little face, and made an effort to say something cheering.

"It bean't all so loansome as what this is, ye know. Theer's t' town o' t'other soide o' t' Abbey, at bottom of t' hill. And from t' windows o' Capt'n Mulgrave's home ye can see roight oop t' river, as pretty a soight as can be, wi' boats a-building, an' red cottages."

"Oh!" said Freda, in a very peaceful voice, "I don't mind the loneliness. I like it best. And I have always lived by the sea, where you could hear the waves till you went to sleep."

"Aye, an' you'll hear 'em here sometimes; fit to split t' owd cliffs oop they cooms crashing in, an' soonding like thoonder. Ye'll have a foin toime here, lass, if ye're fond of t' soond o' t' weaves."

"My father has a yacht too, hasn't he?"

"Aye, an a pretty seeght too, to see it scoodding along. But it goes by steam, it isn't one of yer white booterflies. That sort doan't go fast enough for t' Capt'n."

Freda was no longer listening. They were on the level ground now at the top of the hill. To the right, the fields ran to the edge of the cliff, and there was no building in sight but a poor sort of farm-house, with a pond in front of it, and a few rather dilapidated outhouses round about. But on the left hand hedged off from the road by a high stone wall, and standing in the middle of a field, was the ruined Abbey church, now near enough for Freda to see the tracery left in the windows, and the still perfect turrets of the East end, and of the North transept pointing to heaven, unmindful of the decay of the old altars, and of the old faith that raised them.

Barnabas looked at her intent young face, the great burning eyes, which seemed to be overwhelmed with a strange sorrow.

"Pretty pleace, this owd abbey of ours, isn't it?" said he with all the pride of ownership.

"It's beautiful," said Freda hoarsely, "it makes me want to cry."

Now the rough farmer could understand sentiment about the old ruin; considering as he did that the many generations of Protestant excursionists who had picknicked in it had purged it pretty clear of the curse of popery, he loved it himself with a free conscience.

"Aye," said he, "there's teales aboot it too, for them as loikes to believe 'em. Ah've heard as there were another Abbey here, afore this one, an' not near so fine, wheer there was a leady, an Abbess, Ah think they called her. An' she was a good leady, kind to t' poor, an' not so much to be bleamed for being a Papist, seeing those were dreadful toimes when there was no Protestants. An' they do seay (mahnd, Ah'm not seaying Ah believe it, not being inclined to them soart o' superstitious notions myself) they say how on an afternoon when t' soon shines you can see this Saint Hilda, as they call her, standing in one of t' windows over wheer t' Communion table used for to be." Perceiving, however, that Freda was looking more reverently interested than was quite seemly in a mere legend with a somewhat unorthodox flavour about it, Barnabas, who was going to tell her some more stories of the same sort, changed his mind and ended simply: "An' theer's lots more sooch silly feables which sensible fowk doan't trouble their heads with. Whoa then, Prince!"

The cart drew up suddenly in a sort of inclosure of stone walls. To the right was an ancient and broken stone cross, on a circular flight of rude and worn steps; to the left, a stone-built lodge, a pseudo-Tudor but modern erection, was built over a gateway, the wrought-iron gates of which were shut. In front, a turnstile led into a churchyard. Barnabas got down and pulled the lodge-bell, which gave a startlingly loud peal.

"That yonder," said he, pointing over the wall towards the churchyard, in which Freda could dimly see a shapeless mass of building and a squat, battlemented tower, "is Presterby Choorch. An' this," he continued, as an old woman came out of the lodge and unlocked the gate, "is owd Mary Sarbutt, an she's as deaf as a poast. Now, hark ye, missie," and he held out his hand to help Freda down, "Ah can't go no further with ye, but ye're all reeght now. Joost go oop along t' wall to t' left, streight till ye coom to t' house, an' pull t' bell o' t' gate an' Mrs. Bean, or happen Crispin himself will coom an' open to ye."

The fact was that Barnabas did not for a moment entertain the idea that Captain Mulgrave would have the heart to leave his newly-recovered daughter, and the farmer meant to come up to the Abbey-house in a day or two and let him know quietly that he had nothing to fear from him as long as he proved a good father to the little lass. But just now Barnabas felt shy of showing himself again, and he shook his head when Freda begged him to come a little way further with her. For a glance through the gates at the house showed her such a bare, gaunt, cheerless building that she began to feel frightened and miserable.

"Noa, missie, Ah woan't coom in," said Barnabas, who seemed to have grown both shyer and more deferential when he had landed the young lady at the gates of the big house; "but Ah wish ye ivery happiness, an' if Ah meay mak' so bawld, Ah'll shak' honds wi' ye, and seay good-bye."

Freda with the tears coming, wrung his hand in both hers, and watched him through the gates while he turned the horse, got up in his place in the cart and drove away.

"Barnabas! Barnabas!" she cried aloud.

But the gates were locked, and the old woman, without one word of question or of direction, had gone back into the lodge. Freda turned, blinded with tears, and began to make her way slowly towards the house.

Nothing could be more desolate, more bare, more dreary, than the approach. An oblong, rectangular space, shut in by high stone walls, and without a single shrub or tree, lay between her and the building. Half-way down, to the right, a pillared gateway led to the stables, which were very long and low, and roofed with red tiles. This bit of colour, however, was now hidden by the snow, which lay also, in a smooth sheet, over the whole inclosure. Freda kept close to the left-hand wall, as she had been told to do, her heart sinking within her at every step.

At last, when she had come very near to the façade of the house, which filled the bottom of the inclosure from end to end, a cry burst from her lips. It was shut up, unused, deserted, and roofless. What had once been the front-door, with its classic arch over the top, was now filled up with boards strengthened by bars of iron. The rows of formal, stately Jacobian windows were boarded up, and seemed to turn her sick with a sense of hideous deformity, like eye-sockets without eyes. The sound of her voice startled a great bird which had found shelter in the moss-grown embrasure of one of the windows. Flapping its wings it flew out and wheeled in the air above her.

Shocked, chilled, bewildered, Freda crept back along the front of the house, feeling the walls, from which the mouldy stucco fell in flakes at her touch, and listening vainly for some sound of life to guide her.

CHAPTER VII.

FREDA MULGRAVE was superstitious. While she was groping her way along the front of the dismantled house, she heard a bell tolling fitfully and faintly, and the sound seemed to come from the sea. She flew instantly to the fantastic conclusion that Saint Hilda, in heaven, was ringing the bell of her old church on earth to comfort her in her sore trouble.

"Saint Hilda was always good to wanderers," she thought. And the next moment her heart sprang up with a great leap of joy, for her hand, feeling every excrescence along the wall, had at last touched the long swinging handle of a rusty bell.

Freda pulled it, and there was a hoarse clang. She heard a man's footsteps upon a flagged court-yard, and a rough masculine voice asked:

"Who's that at this time of night?"

"It is Captain Mulgrave's daughter. And oh! take me in; I am tired, tired."

The gate was unbolted and one side was opened, enabling the girl to pass in. The man closed the gate, and lifted a lantern he carried so as to throw the light on Freda's face.

"So you're the Captain's daughter, you say?"

"Yes."

Freda looked at him, with tender eyes full of anxiety and inquiry. He was a tall and rather thickset man with very short greyish hair and a little unshaved stubble on his chin. Her face fell.

"I thought——" she faltered.

"Thought what, miss?"

There was a pause. Then she asked:

"Who are *you*?"

She uttered the words slowly, under her breath.

"I am your servant, ma'am."

"*My* servant—you mean my father's?"

"It is the same thing, is it not?"

"Oh, then you are Crispin Bean!"

The man seemed surprised.

"How did you know my name?"

"They told me about you."

"What did they tell you?"

"That you were a 'rough-looking customer.'"

The man laughed a short, grim laugh, which showed no amusement.

"Well, yes; I suppose they were about right. But who were 'they'?"

"The people at Oldcastle Farm."

The man stopped short just as, after leading her along a wide, stone-paved entry, between the outer wall and the side of the house, he turned into a large square court-yard.

"Oh!" he said, and lifting his lantern again, he subjected the young lady to a second close scrutiny. "So you've been making friends with those vermin."

Freda did not answer for a moment. Presently she said, in a stifled voice:

"I am not able to choose my friends."

"You mean that you haven't got any? Poor creature, poor creature, that's not far from the truth, I suppose. That father of yours didn't treat you over well, or consider you over much, did he?"

Freda grew cold, and her crutch rattled on the stones.

"What do you mean? '*Didn't* treat me well'!" she whispered. "He will, I am sure he will, when he sees me, knows me."

"Oh, no, you're mistaken. He's dead."

Freda did not utter a sound, did not move. She remained transfixed, benumbed, stupefied by the awful intelligence.

"It isn't true! It can't be true!" she whispered at last, with dry lips. "Barnabas saw him to-day—just now."

"He was alive two hours ago. He went out this afternoon, came in in a great state of excitement and went up to his room. Presently I heard a report, burst open the door, and found him dead—shot through the head."

"Dead!" repeated Freda hoarsely.

She could not believe it. All the dreams, which she had cherished up to the last moment in spite of disappointments and disillusions, of a tender and loving father whom her affection and dutiful obedience should reconcile to a world which had treated him harshly, were in a moment dashed to the ground.

"Dead!"

It was the knell of all her hopes, all her girlish happiness. Forlorn, friendless, utterly alone, she was stranded upon this unknown corner of the world, in a cheerless house, with no one to offer her even the comfort of a kindly pressure of the hand. The man seemed sorry for her. He stamped on the ground impatiently, as if her grief distressed and annoyed him.

"Come, come," he said. "You haven't lost much in losing him. I know all about it; he never went to see you all these years, and didn't care a jot whether you lived or died, as far as any one could see. And it's all nonsense to pretend you're sorry, you know. How can you be sorry for a father you don't remember?"

"Oh," said Freda, with a sob, "can't you understand? You can love a person without knowing him, just as we love God, whom we can never see till we die."

"Well, but I suppose you love God, because you think He's good to you."

"We believe He is, even when He allows things to happen to us which seem cruel. And my father being, as I am afraid he was, an unhappy man, was perhaps afraid of making me unhappy too. And he did send for me at last, remember."

"Yes, in a fit of annoyance over something—I forget what."

"How do you know that he hadn't really some other motive in his heart?" said Freda, down whose cheeks the tears were fast rolling. "He was a stern man, everybody says, who didn't show his feelings. So that at last he grew perhaps ashamed to show them."

"More likely hadn't got any worth speaking of," said the man gruffly.

"It's not very nice or right of you to speak ill of your master, when he's de-ad," quavered Freda.

"Well, it's very silly of you to make such a fuss about him when he's de-ad," mimicked the man.

Although he spoke without much feeling of his late master, and although he was somewhat uncouth of speech, manner and appearance, Freda did not dislike this man. As might have been expected, she confounded bluntness with honesty in the conventional manner. Therefore she bore even his little jibes without offence. There was a pause, however, after his last words. Then he asked, rather curiously:

"Come, honestly, what is your reason for taking his part through thick and thin like this? Come," he repeated, getting for the moment no answer, "what is it?"

Freda hesitated, drying her eyes furtively.

"Don't you see," she said, tremulously, "that it is my only consolation now to think the very, very best of him?"

The man, instead of answering, turned from her abruptly, and signed to her with his hand to follow him. This she did; and they passed round one side of the court-yard under a gallery, supported by a colonnade, and entering the house, went through a wide, low hall, into an apartment to the right at the front of the building. It was a pretty room, with a low ceiling handsomely moulded, panelled walls, and an elaborately carved wooden mantelpiece, which had been a good deal knocked about. The room had been furnished with solid comfort, if without much regard to congruity, a generation or so back; and the mahogany arm-chairs having been since shrouded in voluminous chintz covers with a pattern of large flowers on a dark ground, the room looked warm and cheerful. Tea was laid on the table for two persons. Freda's sharp eyes noted this circumstance at once. She turned round quickly.

"Who is this tea for?" she asked.

"Captain Mulgrave's death was not discovered until it was ready."

"But it was laid for two. Was it for you also?"

"Yes."

Freda's face fell.

"You think it was derogatory to his dignity to have his meals with me?"

"Oh, no, no indeed," said Freda blushing. "I knew at once, when you said you were a servant, that it was only a way of speaking. You were an officer on board his ship, of course?"

"Yes," said he.

"But I had hoped," said Freda wilfully, "that he had expected me, and had tea made ready for me and him together."

"Ah!" said the man shortly. "Sit down," he went on, pointing brusquely to a chair without looking at her, "I'll send Mrs. Bean to you; she must find a room for you somewhere, I suppose."

"For to-night, yes, if you please. Mrs. Bean—that is your wife?"

He nodded and went out, shutting the door.

Freda heard him calling loudly "Nell, Nell!" in a harsh, authoritative voice, as he went down the passage.

She thought she should be glad to be alone, to have an opportunity to think. But she could not. The series of exciting adventures through which she had passed since she left the quiet convent life had benumbed her, so that this awful discovery of her father's sudden death, though it agitated her did not impress her with any sense of reality. When she tried to picture him lying dead upstairs, she failed altogether; she must see him by-and-by, kiss his cold face; and then she thought that she would be better able to pray that she might meet him in heaven.

It seemed to her that she had been left alone for hours when a bright young woman's voice, speaking rather querulously, reached her ears. Freda guessed, before she saw Mrs. Bean, that her father's fellow-officer or servant (she was uncertain what to call him) had married beneath him. However, when the door opened, it revealed, if not a lady of the highest refinement, a very pleasant-looking, plump little woman, with fair hair and bright eyes, who wore a large apron but no cap, and who looked altogether like an important member of the household, accustomed to have her own way unquestioned.

"Dear me, and is that the little lady?" she asked, in a kind, motherly voice, encircling the girl with a rounded arm of matronly protection. "Bless her poor little heart, she looks half-perished. Crispin," she went on, in a distant tone, which seemed to betray that she and her husband had been indulging in a little discussion, "go and put the kettle on while I take the young lady upstairs. Come along, my dear. I'll get you some hot water and some dry clothes, and in two-twos I'll have you as cosy as can be."

Mrs. Bean looked a little worried, but she was evidently not the woman to take to heart such a trifle as a suicide in the house, as long as things went all right in the kitchen, and none of the chimneys smoked. Crispin, who seemed to have little trust in her discretion, gave her arm a rough shake of warning as she left the room with the young lady. Mrs. Bean, therefore, kept silence until she and her charge got upstairs. Then she popped her head over the banisters to see that Crispin was out of hearing, and proceeded to unbend in conversation, being evidently delighted to have somebody fresh to speak to.

CHAPTER VIII.

"OH," began Mrs. Bean, with a fat and comfortable sigh, "I am glad to have you here, I declare. Ever since the Captain told me, in his short way, that you were coming, I've been that anxious to see you, you might have been my own sister."

"That was very good of you," said Freda, who was busily taking in all the details of the house, the wide, shallow stairs, low ceilings, and oaken panelling; the air of neglect which hung about it all; the draughts which made her shiver in the corridors and passages. She compared it with the farm-house she had just left, so much less handsome, so much more comfortable. How wide these passages were! The landing at the top of the staircase was like a room, with a long mullioned window and a wide window-seat. But it was all bare, cold, smelling of mould and dust.

"Isn't this part of the house lived in?" asked Freda.

"Well, yes and no. The Captain lives in it—at least *did* live in it," she corrected, lowering her voice and with a hasty glance around. "No one else. This house would hold thirty people, easy, so that three don't fill it very well."

"But doesn't it take a lot of work to keep it clean?"

"It never is kept clean. What's the good of sweeping it up for the rats?" asked Mrs. Bean comfortably. "I and a girl who comes in to help just keep our own part clean and the two rooms the Captain uses, and the rest has to go. If the Captain had minded dust he'd have had to keep servants; I don't consider myself a servant, you know," she continued with a laugh, "and I'm not going to slave myself to a skeleton for people that save a sixpence where they might spend a pound."

It would have taken a lot of slaving to make a skeleton of Mrs. Bean, Freda thought.

They passed round the head of the staircase and into a long gallery which overlooked the court-yard. It was panelled and hung with dark and dingy portraits in frames which had once been gilt.

"Does any one live in this part?" asked Freda, shivering.

Mrs. Bean's candle threw alarming shadows on the walls. The mullioned window, which ran from end to end of the gallery, showed a dreary outlook of dark walls surrounding a stretch of snow.

"Well, no," admitted her guide reluctantly. "The fact is there isn't another room in the house that's fit to put anybody into; they've been unused so long that they're reeking with damp, most of them; some of the windows are broken. And so I thought I'd put you into the Abbot's room. It's a long way from the rest of us, but it's had a fire in it once or twice lately, when the Captain has had young Mulgrave here. It's a bit gloomy looking and old fashioned, but you mustn't mind that."

Freda shivered again. If the room she was to have was more gloomy than the way to it, a mausoleum would be quite as cheerful.

"The Abbot's room!" exclaimed Freda. "Why is it called that?"

"Why, this house wasn't all built at the same time, you know. There's a big stone piece at this end that was built earliest of all. It's very solid and strong, and they say it was the Abbot's house. Then in Henry the Eighth's time it was turned into a gentleman's house, in what they call the Tudor style. They built two new wings, and carried the gallery all round the three sides. A hundred and fifty years later a banqueting room was built, making the last side of the square; but it was burnt down, and now there's nothing left of it but the outside walls of the front and sides."

This explained to Freda the desolate appearance the house had presented as she approached it. The deep interest she felt in this, the second venerable house she had been in since her arrival in England, began to get the better of her alarm at its gloominess. But at the angle of the house, where the gallery turned sharply to the right, Mrs. Bean unlocked a door, and introduced her to a narrow stone passage which was like a charnel-house.

"This," said Mrs. Bean with some enthusiasm, "is the very oldest part; and I warrant you'll not find such another bit of masonry, still habitable, mind, in any other house in England!"

Was it habitable? Freda doubted it. The walls of the passage were of great blocks of rough stone. It was so narrow that the two women could scarcely walk abreast. They passed under a pointed arch of rough-hewn stone, and came presently to the end of the passage, where a narrow window, deeply splayed, threw a little line of murky light on to the boards of the floor. On the right was a low and narrow Gothic doorway, with the door in perfect preservation. Mrs. Bean opened it by drawing back a rusty bolt, and ushered Freda, with great pride, into a room which seemed fragrant with the memories of a bygone age. Freda looked round almost in terror. Surely the Abbot must still be lurking about, and would start out presently, in dignified black habit, cowl and sandals, and haughtily demand the reason of her intrusion! For here was the very wide fireplace, reaching four feet from the ground, and without any mantelshelf, where fires had burned for holy Abbot or episcopal guest four hundred years ago. Here were the narrow windows deeply splayed like the one outside from which the prosperous monks had looked out over their wide pasture-lands and well-stocked coverts.

Even in the furniture there was little that was incongruous with the building. The roughly plastered walls were hung with tapestry much less carefully patched and mended than the hangings at Oldcastle Farm. The floor was covered by an old carpet of harmoniously undistinguishable pattern. The rough but solid chairs of unpolished wood, with worn leather seats; the ancient press, long and low, which served at one end as a washhand-stand, and at the other as a dressing-table; a large writing-table, which might have stood in the scriptorium of the Abbey itself, above all, the enormous four-poster bedstead, with faded tapestry to match the walls, and massive worm-eaten carvings of Scriptural subjects: all these combined to make the chamber unlike any that Freda had ever seen.

"There!" said Mrs. Bean, as she plumped down the candlestick upon the writing table, "you've never slept in a room like this before!"

"No, indeed I haven't," answered Freda, who would willingly have exchanged fourteenth century tapestry and memories of dead Abbots for an apartment a little more draught-tight.

"Ah! There's plenty of gentlemen with as many thousands as the Captain had hundreds, would give their eyes for the Abbot's guest chamber in Sea-Mew Abbey. Now I'll just leave you while I fetch some hot water and some dry clothes. They won't fit you very well, you being thin and me fat, but we're not much in the fashion here. Do you mind being left without a light till I come back?"

Freda did mind very much, but she would not own to it. Just as Mrs. Bean was going away with the candle, however, she sprang towards her, and asked, in a trembling voice:

"Mrs. Bean, may I see him—my father?"

The housekeeper gave a great start.

"Bless me, no, child!" she said in a frightened voice. "Who'd ever have thought of your asking such a thing! It's no sight for you, my dear," she added hurriedly.

Freda paused for a moment. But she still held Mrs. Bean's sleeve, and when that lady had recovered her breath, she said:

"That was my poor father's room, to the right when we reached the top of the stairs, wasn't it?"

Again the housekeeper started.

"Why, how did you know that?" she asked breathlessly.

"I saw you look towards the door on the left like this," said Freda, imitating a frightened glance.

Mrs. Bean shook her head, puzzled and rather solemn.

"Those sharp eyes of yours will get you into trouble if you don't take care," she said, "unless you've got more gumption than girls of your age are usually blest with. We womenfolks," she went on sententiously, "are always thought more of when we don't seem over-bright. Take that from me as a word of advice, and if ever you see or hear more than you think you can keep to yourself, why, come and tell *me*—but nobody else."

And Mrs. Bean with a friendly nod, and a kindly, rough pat on the cheek which was almost a slap, left the girl abruptly, and went out of the room.

But this warning, after all the mysterious experiences of the last two days, was more than Freda could bear without question. She waited, stupefied, until she could no longer hear the sound of Mrs. Bean's retreating footsteps, and then, with one hasty glance round her which took in frowning bedstead, yawning fireplace and dim windows, she groped her way to the door, which was unfastened, and fled out along the stone passage. Her crutch seemed to raise strange echoes, which filled her with alarm. She hurt herself against the rough, projecting stones of the wall as she ran. The gallery-door was open: like a mouse she crept through, becoming suddenly afraid lest Mrs. Bean should hear her. For she wanted to see her father's body. A horrible suspicion had struck her; these people seemed quite unconcerned at his death; did they know more about it than they told her? Had he really shot himself, or had he been murdered? She thought if she could see his dead face that she would know.

Tipity-tap went her crutch and her little feet along the boards of the gallery. The snow in the court-yard outside still threw a white glare on the dingy portraits; she dared not look full at them, lest their eyes should follow her in the darkness. For she did not feel that the dwellers in this gloomy house had been kith and kin to her. She reached the landing, and was frightened by the scampering of mice behind the panelling. Still as a statue she stood outside the door of her father's room, her heart beating loudly, her eyes fixed on the faint path of light on the floor, listening. She heard no sound above or below: summoning her courage, she turned the handle, which at first refused to move under her clammy fingers, and peeped into the room.

A lamp was burning on a table in the recess of the window, but the curtains were not drawn. There was a huge bed in the room, upon which her eyes at once rested, while she held her breath. The curtains were closely drawn! Freda felt that her limbs refused to carry her. She had never yet looked upon the dead, and the horror of the thought, suddenly overpowered her. Her eyes wandered round the room; she noted, even more clearly than she would have done at a time when her mind was free, the disorder with which clothes, papers and odds and ends of all sorts, were strewn about the furniture and the floor. On two chairs stood an open portmanteau, half-filled. She could not understand it.

Just as, recovering her self-command, she was advancing towards the bed, with her right hand raised to draw back the curtain, she heard a man's footsteps approaching outside, and turned round in terror. The door was flung suddenly open, and a man entered.

"Who's in here?" he asked, sharply.

"It is I," said Freda hoarsely, but boldly. "I have come to see my father. And I will see him too. If you don't let me, I shall believe you have killed him."

She almost shrieked these last words in her excitement. But the intruder, in whom she recognised the man she knew as Crispin Bean, took her hand very gently and led her out of the room.

CHAPTER IX.

FREDA was so easily led by kindness that when, not heeding her passionate outburst, Crispin pushed her gently out of the room, she made no protest either by word or action. He left her alone on the landing while he went back to get a light, and when he rejoined her, it was with a smile of good-humoured tolerance on his rugged face.

"So you think I murdered your father, do you, eh?" he said, as he turned the key in the lock and then put it in his pocket.

"Why don't you let me see him?" asked she, pleadingly.

"I have a good reason, you may be sure. I am not a woman, to act out of mere caprice. That's enough for you. Go downstairs."

Freda obeyed, carrying her crutch and helping herself down by the banisters.

"Why don't you use your crutch?" called out Crispin, who was holding the lamp over the staircase head, and watching her closely. "If you can do without it now, I should think you could do without it always?"

He spoke in rather a jeering tone. At least Freda thought so, and she was up in arms in a moment. Turning, and leaning on the banisters, she looked up at him with a gleam of daring spirit in her red-brown eyes.

"It's a caprice, you may be sure," she answered slowly. "I am not a man, to act upon mere reason."

Crispin gave a great roar of derisive laughter, shocking the girl, who hopped down the rest of the stairs as fast as possible and ran, almost breathless, into the room she had been in before. Mrs. Bean was bringing in some cold meat and eggs, and she turned, with an alarmed exclamation at sight of her.

"Bless the girl!" she cried. "Why didn't you wait till I came to you? I have a bundle of dry clothes waiting outside, and now you'll catch your death of cold, sitting in those wet things!"

"Oh, no, I sha'n't," said Freda, "we were not brought up to be delicate at the convent, and it was only the edge of my dress that was wet."

Mrs. Bean was going to insist on sending her upstairs again, when Crispin, who had followed them into the room, put an end to the discussion by drawing a chair to the table and making the girl sit down in it.

"Have you had your tea?" asked Freda.

"I don't want any tea," said he gruffly. "I've got to pack up my things; I'm going away to-night."

"Going away!" echoed Freda rather regretfully.

"Well, why shouldn't I? I'm sure you'll be very happy here without me." And, without further ceremony, he left the room.

Mrs. Bean made a dart at the table, swooped upon a plate and a knife which were not being used, and with the air of one labouring under a sudden rush of business, bustled out after him.

There was a clock in the room, but it was not going. It seemed to Freda that she was left a very long time by herself. Being so tired that she was restless, she wandered round and round the room, and thought at last that she would go in search of Crispin. So she opened the door softly, stepped out into the wide hall, and by the dim light of a small oil lamp on a bracket, managed to find her way across the wide hall to the back-door leading into the court-yard. This door, however, was locked. To the left was another door leading, as Freda knew, into Mrs. Bean's quarters. This also was locked. She went back therefore to the room she had left, the door of which she had closed behind her. To her astonishment, she found this also locked. This circumstance seemed so strange that she was filled with alarm; and not knowing what to do, whether to call aloud in the hope that Mrs. Bean or Crispin would hear her, or to go round the hall, trying all the doors once more, she sat down on the lowest steps of the staircase listening and considering the situation.

A slight noise above her head made her turn suddenly, and looking up she saw peering at her through the banisters of the landing, an ugly, withered face. Utterly horrorstruck, and convinced that the apparition was superhuman, Freda, without a word or a cry, sank into a frightened heap at the bottom of the stairs, and hid her eyes. She heard no further sound; and when she looked up again, the face was gone. But the shock she had received was so great that it made her desperate; getting up from her crouching position, she sped across the hall, frightened by the echoes of her crutch and her own feet, and threw herself with all her force against the great door, making the chain swing and rattle.

"What's that?" cried Mrs. Bean's cheery voice in the distance.

And in a few moments the door leading to the kitchen was opened, and the buxom housekeeper appeared.

"Oh, Mrs. Bean," cried Freda, throwing herself into her arms and speaking in a voice hoarse with fear, "this house is haunted!"

"Bless the poor child! you're overtired, and you fancy things, my dear," she said soothingly. "All these old places are full of strange noises, but you'll soon get used to them."

"But *faces*! I saw a face, a dreadful face, with long sharp teeth like a death's head; it was looking at me through the banisters, up there!"

And poor Freda, with her head still buried in Mrs. Bean's plump shoulder, pointed upwards with her finger.

"Oh, no, my dear, you didn't. It was only your fancy. What you want is to go to bed, and after a good night's rest you'll see no more death's heads."

Mrs. Bean's manner was so very quiet and matter-of-fact, and she took the account of the appearance so unemotionally, that it occurred to Freda to ask:

"Haven't you heard of that face being seen before?"

"Well," said the housekeeper, rather taken aback, "I believe I have heard something about it."

"And the doors, why do they lock of themselves?"

"Oh, that's very simple," answered the housekeeper quickly. "That's a patent invented by the Captain for the greater security of the house when he didn't live here himself. I will show you how to open them."

She crossed to the door of the dining-room, followed by Freda. But it seemed to the girl that she listened a few moments, before attempting to open it. Then she turned what looked like a little ornamental button above the keyhole, and the door opened.

"That's how it's done; you see it's perfectly simple."

"Ye-es," said Freda, "but it all seems to me very strange."

Mrs. Bean laughed, and wanted the girl to amuse herself with a book while she cleared away the tea-things.

But no sooner was the housekeeper's broad back turned than Freda was off her chair in a moment, and out of the kitchen to a door which opened into the court-yard. As this door had no secret bolt, she was speedily outside, under the gallery.

Fancying, that she heard voices to the left, Freda turned in that direction, and presently saw Crispin standing ankle-deep in the snow, looking up at the gallery above.

"Were you talking to some one, Crispin?" she cried.

He started at the sound of her voice, and came towards her with impatient steps.

"What the d——l are you doing out here?" he asked angrily, with a stamp of his foot on the ground.

"I came out to talk to you," she answered. "I sha'n't catch cold."

"You'll catch something worse than cold if you come wandering out here at all hours of the night," muttered Crispin roughly. "Nell must keep you indoors."

He came through the sheltered colonnade, stamping the snow off his feet.

"You're a very disagreeable man, Crispin," said Freda, watching him gravely. "You must have been very good to my father for him to have kept you about him so long. It shows," she went on triumphantly, "that he must have been much more amiable than they say. Do you know I think you only talk against him to tease me. But it is horrible, now that he's dead."

Her voice sank on the last word, and the tears started again.

When Crispin answered, which was not at once, his voice was scarcely so harsh as before, though he spoke rather scoffingly.

"Women are always full of fancies. I don't wonder your father couldn't stand them!"

It was Freda's turn to laugh now.

"Oh," she cried, "then I knew him better than you after all. For he loved one woman so well that he could never bear to look at another after she died. And he left his own daughter among women, nothing but women. And I believe that all those years he wouldn't see me because he thought I could never be good enough for her daughter. I was lame, you see," she added softly.

There was a long, long pause. Freda had managed to get on the right side of rough Crispin. For he suddenly startled her by taking her in his right arm with a sweeping embrace which nearly took her off her feet, while he said huskily:

"Come in, there's a dear child; you're cold. You're quite right, I'll be good to you for the sake of—— Well, for your own sake!"

He half led, half carried her along under the gallery and into the house. Mrs. Bean, who was standing at the back door with rather an anxious look upon her face, seemed relieved to see that they returned in amity. Crispin took the girl into a long, low-ceilinged room, where the furniture, in holland bags, was stacked up against the walls. He led her before a large oil-painting of a lady, the charm of whose gracious beauty, even the old-fashioned fourth-rate portrait-painter had not been able wholly to destroy.

"I suppose you can guess who that is," said Crispin.

"My mother," said Freda softly.

"I believe the Captain thought a lot of this picture once. But for the last few years his memory had grown a bit dim, and he remembered bitter things better than sweet ones."

Freda drew a little nearer to Crispin. She perceived by his tone how strong the sympathy had been between him and her father. She gave a little sigh, and they instinctively turned to each other and exchanged glances of growing liking and confidence as they went down the long room and crossed the hall to the dining-room. Crispin turned up the lamp, and was about to refill his pipe when it occurred to him to turn to the girl and say:

"You won't be able to stand this indoors, I suppose?"

"Oh, yes, I shall. They smoked all the time in the kitchen, at the 'Barley Mow.'"

"The 'Barley Mow,' eh? How did you get there?"

Freda told him the whole story of her journey, her sojourn at the inn, the mysterious character they gave her father.

When she mentioned her friend who was connected with the government, Crispin grew very attentive, and asked for a minute description of him, at the end of which he said: "The scoundrel! That's the fellow who was sneaking about here this afternoon. If I'd guessed——"

He did not finish his sentence, but he looked so black that Freda hastened to get off the unpleasant subject, and rushed into a description of her adventures at Oldcastle Farm. This, however, proved even less pleasing. Crispin listened with a frown on his face to her account of the kindness of the Heritages, and at last broke out into open impatience.

"Mind," said he sharply, "if those two young cubs come carnying about here while I'm away—as they will do, my word on it—you are not to let them inside the door on any pretence, remember that."

"I wouldn't let Robert in," said Freda decidedly.

"No, nor Dick, either."

"I should let Dick in," said Freda softly.

Crispin sat back in his chair to look at her face, and perceived upon it a rosy red flush.

"Now look here," he said, like one trembling on the borders of a great outburst of passion, "if you let Dick Heritage come fooling about you here, I'll shoot him through the head. Now you understand."

Freda looked up with a sudden flash of haughtiness.

"I am going back to the convent, Crispin, and these gentlemen are nothing to me. But if I were going to stay in this house, I should see whom I liked, for I should be the mistress here."

If she had stabbed him he would not have been more surprised. He held his pipe in his hand, and stared at her, unable at first to find words. She, on her side, felt very uncomfortable as soon as the outburst had escaped her. She felt that a confession had slipped out against her will, and she hung her head, and looked into the fire, hoping that the glow would hide her flaming cheeks.

"So you would be mistress here, would you?" he said. "And you intend to go back to the convent? And I suppose you think your father's wishes nothing."

"I don't know what they were; and I shall never know now!"

"Well, I'll tell you. His wishes were that you should remain here, and call yourself mistress if you like, while I go away to manage his property abroad for him."

"But, Crispin, what could I do here? I should be miserable. I should like a nun's life, but not a hermit's!"

"Oh, well, you'll get used to it. Your father had a troop of pensioners in the town here: you will have them to look after."

"Crispin," she said suddenly after a pause, in a whisper, "who do you think it was that killed Blewitt?"

Crispin was rather startled by the question.

"Well," he asked in his turn, looking stolidly at the fire, "who did Barnabas Ugthorpe think it was?"

"Oh," said Freda quickly, "he was wrong, altogether wrong. I told him so."

"And supposing he had been right, altogether right, your father would be a murderer."

Freda bent her head, but said nothing.

"What do you say to that?"

The girl burst out fierily:

"Why, that he was not a murderer! he was not, he was not! And I wouldn't believe it if—if everybody in England had been there!"

She kept her head up, and looked at him steadily, her eyes flashing defiance. After a few moments he got up.

"You're tired, and you're very silly," he said, huskily.

And, with a nod, but without again looking at her he left the room, as Mrs. Bean came in with a candle.

CHAPTER X.

"YOU'LL be glad to go to bed, I dare say, my dear," said the housekeeper. "If you hear any noises in the night, don't be afraid; this old house is full of them. Good-night."

Freda fled across the hall and hopped up the stairs.

Oh! How long that gallery seemed, skim over the floor as she might! The candle smoked and flared and guttered in her hand, and the boards creaked, and the musty smell seemed to choke her. The row of stately carved oak chairs, ranged along the wall on one side, seemed to be set ready for the midnight hour when the faded ladies and the sombre gentlemen should come down from their frames and hold ghostly converse there. She ran along the stone passage to the door of her room, and threw it open suddenly.

A man sprang up from his knees before the wide, open grate, in which a wood fire now burned. The girl, no longer mistress of herself in her fright and excitement, uttered a cry.

"It's all right," said the rough voice which had already begun to grow familiar to her, "I thought you'd like a fire. So I brought some sticks, and a log. It's cold here after France, I expect. Anyhow, the blaze makes it look more cheerful."

Freda was touched.

"Oh, thank you—so very much! How kind of you."

"Stuff! Kind! You're mistress here now, you know, as you said; and one must make the mistress comfortable."

He spoke in a jeering tone, but Freda did not mind that now.

"I wish," she said, looking wistfully at the blazing log, "that you were going to stay here, Crispin."

He gave one of his short, hard laughs.

"I should get spoilt for work," he said. "You'd make a ladies'-man of me. Sha'n't see you again. Good-night."

Freda held out her hand, and he held it a moment in his, while a gleam almost of tenderness passed over his seamed and rugged face. Then he gave her fingers a sudden, rough squeeze, which left her red girl's hand for a minute white and helpless.

"Good-night," he then said again, shortly and as if indifferently. "If I come into these parts again, I'll give you a look in."

He left her hardly time to murmur "good-night" in answer, before he was out of the room. He put his head in again immediately, however, to say "Draw the bolt of the door, and you'll be all right."

Freda obeyed this direction at once, with another little quiver of the heart. But Crispin's kindness had so warmed her that what now chiefly troubled her was the fact that she would see no more of him for an indefinite time. The strongest proof of the confidence he had inspired in her was the fact that she accepted implicitly his assurance as to her father's wishes, and resolved to make no attempt to return to the convent. Indeed, the last three days had been so full of excitement and adventure that the old, calm years seemed to have been passed by some other person.

Freda's last thought as she fell asleep, watching the dancing light of the fire on the roughly white-washed beams of the ceiling, was, however, neither of quiet nuns at their prayers in the convent by the sea, nor of Crispin Bean with his rugged face and hard voice, but of Oldcastle Farm and one of its occupants.

The girl was tired out; so utterly weary that she was ready to lie like a log till morning. But presently she began to dream, with the leaden drowsiness of a person in whom some outward disturbance struggles with fatigue, of thunder and battling crowds of men. And then she started into wakefulness, and found that the fire had burnt low, and that men's loud voices were disturbing her rest. They seemed to come, muffled by the massive boards between, from a chamber under hers; they died away into faintness, and she was so overpowered with fatigue that she would have dropped to sleep again almost without troubling herself, when one voice suddenly broke out above the murmur. It was loud and shrill, and high-pitched, a voice Freda had never heard before. She could hear the words it uttered:

"Ye maun stay, ye maun stay. We can't get on wi'out ye. Do ye want us to starve?"

And a chorus of evidently assenting murmurs followed. The voices dropped again, and again the listening girl's attention relaxed, as sleep got the better of her senses. But suddenly she was aroused again, this time by sounds which came from behind the head of the bed, and were so plain that they seemed to be in the very room. Sounds as of a man's footsteps coming up a stone staircase, coming up unsteadily, with many pauses. Sounds, too, as of heavy weights being dragged up, and of suppressed laughter and jeers.

"Eh, but tha's gotten aboot as much as tha' can carry, eh, Crispin?" said one voice.

"Tha' couldn't climb oop a mast to-night, Crispin," said another, during the laughter which succeeded the first speech.

The voice of the man who was on the stairs answered, in low and husky tones. Although he was the nearest to her, Freda could not distinguish what he said, except the word "hush." Then she heard a mumbling sound, like the drawing back of a sliding door, and then the dragging of some heavy weight over the boards, and the opening of a window. Presently the man came back, went down the stone steps, and re-ascended in the same manner as before. This happened three or four times, until the voices below died gradually away, and the sounds ceased. Not until long after all was quiet did Freda fall asleep again, and for the remainder of the night her rest was troubled by all sorts of wild dreams.

Next morning, as a consequence of her broken night's rest, she did not wake until the housekeeper knocked loudly at the door. Springing up with a sudden rush of confused memories through her brain, Freda ran to the door, drew back the bolt, and pulled Mrs. Bean into the room.

"Oh," she cried, "this is a dreadful house; how can you stay in it? It is haunted, or——"

Mrs. Bean interrupted her with a peculiar expression on her face.

"Didn't I tell you to take no notice of anything you heard?" she asked quietly. "What does it matter to you what goes on outside your door, while you're locked safe inside?"

"But I want to know——" began Freda.

Again Mrs. Bean cut her short.

"Didn't they teach you, in the place you came from, that curiosity was the worst sin a woman can have?" she asked drily. "A wise woman doesn't meddle with anything outside her own business, and especially she does not poke her nose into any business where men only are concerned. I see you've had a fire," she went on in a less severe tone.

"Yes, Crispin made it for me."

Mrs. Bean shook her head good-humouredly.

"You're making a fool of that man. He was to have gone away last night, and he is still hanging about this morning. And it's all because of you, I'm certain. Now make haste and get dressed, for I've got a tiresome day's work before me, and I want to get the breakfast done with as soon as I can."

It was a bright, sunny morning. The numerous windows let in floods of sunshine, the snow outside dazzled the eyes, even the knights and dames in the picture-gallery seemed to be in better spirits. In the dining-room Freda found Crispin, who affected to treat her with marked coldness, and to be grieved that he had had to put off his journey until the following night. Now although she stood in some awe of the housekeeper, Freda had no fear whatever of Crispin; so she very soon opened the dangerous subject.

"Crispin," she began solemnly, "I heard you last night after I was in bed."

"Very likely," he answered quietly.

"There were some men with you."

"Yes, so there were."

"The voices seemed to come from under my room."

"So they did."

"And some one came up the stairs."

He nodded.

"Dragging a heavy weight over the floor," continued she. "And then some one opened a window. And the sounds went on over and over again."

"Quite right. Well?"

"What did it all mean?"

"That I had some of the men from your father's yacht here, and told them all about his death. I suppose you don't wish the yacht sold? It would throw half a dozen men out of work."

"No-o," said Freda. "But——"

"Here's your breakfast," he interrupted, as Mrs. Bean brought a laden tray into the room.

CHAPTER XI.

CRISPIN had breakfasted, but he remained in the room, "to wait," as he said with grim jocularity, "on the mistress of the house." Whenever she tried to bring the talk again to the subject of the noises of the night, he slid away from it in a most skilful manner, so that she could find out nothing from him, and presently got rather a sharp warning about the value of silence. When she again expressed a wish to see her father, too, he answered very shortly, so that she began to understand that Crispin's goodwill did not render him pliable. Mrs. Bean was in the room when she made this last request. She stood up suddenly, with a crumb-brush in her hand, and a look of great annoyance upon her face.

"There'll have to be an inquest!" cried she. "Did you ever think of that?"

And she turned in great agitation to Crispin, who was just lighting his pipe. He only nodded and said quietly:

"Don't you trouble yourself. I've thought of all that. You just put on your bonnet and run down to the town, and tell Eliza Poad that the master's shot himself. Then it will be all over the county in about three quarters of an hour, and the police will have notice, and the coroner will be sent for without any trouble to you. And within two hours Mr. Staynes will come panting up the hill with religious consolation."

"I sha'n't see him, interfering old nuisance!" said Mrs. Bean indignantly.

"No, Miss Freda will. And you, Nell, will go to the undertaker's; go to John Posgate—we owe him a good turn—and tell him you don't want any of his measuring: he's to send a coffin, largest size he makes, up to the house-door by to-night, and leave it there. And then go round to the house of that young doctor that's just come here (he lives in one of the little new red houses on the other side of the bridge past the station) and tell him what has happened. And you will be glad if he will step up at once. That's all."

These details made Freda sick; she retreated, shivering, to the window, and there she perceived a long, much trampled foot-track in the snow across the walled-in garden. She noticed it very particularly, wondering whether it was by this way that the men had entered the house on the preceding evening. Then, as she was by this time alone, she went softly out of the room and upstairs, and turned the handle of the door of her father's room. It opened. She saw, with a wildly-beating heart, that the curtains of the bed were drawn back, and that on it there lay the body of a man.

Suddenly she was lifted off her feet, and carried back from the door of the room.

"Look here," said Crispin drily, as he put her down, "haven't you learnt by this time that it's of no more use to try to circumvent me than to fight the sea? You will see your father when I please and not before. Now go downstairs and wait till the Vicar comes, and tell the old fool just as little as you can help, if you don't want to get yourself or anybody else into trouble."

Freda obeyed, mute and ashamed. She crept downstairs, returned to the dining-room, and fed the hungry birds till the bell sounded. Running out to the court-yard gate, she drew back the two heavy bolts which fastened it. Waiting outside were a lady and gentleman whom she at once guessed to be the Vicar and his wife.

The Reverend Berkley Staynes was generally considered the greatest "character" in Presterby. A member of one of the county families, with a fairly good living and a better private income, he was an autocrat who considered his flock of very small account indeed compared with the well-being of their pastor. Although close upon eighty years of age, and quite unable to perform a tithe of his parish duties, he would never take a curate, partly from motives of economy, and partly because he feared that an assistant might introduce some "crank" of week-day services or early Communion, and wake up some of the parishioners into disconcerting religious activity. Never at any time over-burdened with brains, he had been at one time an exceedingly handsome man, athletic and muscular, and a great encourager of health-giving sports and pastimes. For these former good qualities, and from a natural, loyal conservatism, the good Yorkshire folk bore with him, maintained respectful silence while he droned out his antiquated sermons, and shut their eyes to his inefficiency. Mrs. Staynes belonged to a type of clergyman's wife sufficiently common. She was much younger than her husband, and slavishly devoted to him, giving him the absurd homage which he believed to be his due, and working like a nigger to shield his deficiencies from the public notice.

Something of this was to be guessed even by inexperienced Freda as she opened the gate to them. A tall, but somewhat bent old gentleman, still handsome in his age, with silver-white hair and a good-looking, rather stupid face, dressed well and with scrupulous neatness, stood before her. Behind him rather than at his side was a small, middle-aged woman dressed in what looked like a black pillow-case, a long narrow black cloth jacket and a rusty black hat of the old mushroom shape. She had a fresh-coloured face and a simple-minded smile, and she habitually carried her left hand planted against her waist in a manner which emphasised the undesirable curves in her "stumpy" figure.

52

"H'm, a new servant!" said the Reverend Berkley Staynes, looking searchingly at Freda. "Well, what the Captain wanted more servants for, considering that he never received anybody or kept the place up, I'm sure I don't know! Why don't you wear a cap, young woman?"

"I'm not a servant," said Freda. "I'm Captain Mulgrave's daughter. Will you please come in?"

She led the way, without waiting for any more comments, across the court-yard, through the hall, and into the dining-room; and she noticed as she went how both her visitors peered about them and walked slowly, as if they had not been inside the house before, and were curious about it. In the dining-room they sat down, and the Vicar, glancing round the room inquisitively as he spoke, began a close interrogatory as to Freda's history. His wife looked uncomfortable and he solemn when she mentioned the convent.

"Ah! Bad places, those convents," he said, shaking his head, "nests of laziness and superstition."

"Dear me, yes," said Mrs. Staynes. "But we'll cure you of all that. You shall come to the Sunday school and hear Mr. Staynes talking to the girls; and when you feel pretty firm in the doctrine, we'll have you confirmed."

"Thank you," said Freda.

"I'll come in again myself in a day or two, and perhaps we'll have you round to tea. You'd like to come, I daresay."

"Of course she would," chimed in Mrs. Staynes.

"Thank you," said Freda.

"I think," said the Vicar, rising and moving towards the door, "that I'll go upstairs and just look upon the poor Captain's face again. I feel it my duty to. I wish I could have felt happier about him, but I'm sorry to say he was always deaf to the exhortations of religion."

"I'm afraid you can't see him," said Freda, quietly.

She had had particular injunctions on this point from Crispin, who had foreseen that the Vicar would think it his duty to satisfy his curiosity. As Mr. Staynes persisted, brushing her angrily out of his way, Freda followed him upstairs, and had to point out the door of the death-chamber. The Vicar tried to open it, but it was locked; Freda let him push and shake in vain.

"Can you open it for me, girl?" he was at last constrained to ask.

"I think I could, but I have been told not to. I am sorry, but I cannot help you."

"And pray who is it that has more authority with you than the Vicar of the parish?" asked Mr. Staynes when, finding indignation and expostulation useless, he had to accompany her downstairs.

"Crispin Bean," she answered simply.

"What!" cried the Vicar, almost staggering back. "That drunken ruffian Bean! A disgrace to the neighbourhood! Why, it was enough to keep Christian people away from this house that such a scoundrel was ever allowed about it."

The implied taunt at her dead father incensed Freda as much as the accusations against Crispin.

"I suppose," she said very quietly, "that my father liked scoundrels better than Christian people. I think I do too."

The Vicar drew himself up.

In the midst of his anger at being thwarted, the girl's answer rather tickled him.

"I shall come and have a talk to you, young woman," he said more amiably, "when you're in a better frame of mind. You've had everything against you, and I make allowance for it."

Little Mrs. Staynes, who had listened to the latter part of this conversation in such horror that she had scarcely breath left to play her usual part of chorus, followed her husband out, pausing as she did so to say, in a warning voice:

"Oh, dear child, pray to be forgiven for your conduct to-day."

Freda, who was distressed to the verge of tears by the whole interview, let them out by the big gate, and returned to the house. She was almost frightened to find Crispin in the dining-room, in roars of laughter.

"Well done, little one," he said, as she came in. "That's the way to serve the tract-mongers."

But Freda was shocked.

"What did you hear? Where were you?" she asked in a whisper.

"I heard everything. Never mind where I was; there's many a corner in this house that you will never see."

But the girl shrank away, ill-pleased at his praise.

When the housekeeper returned, she was accompanied by the doctor Crispin had sent her for, and he and Mrs. Bean went upstairs at once. As soon as she heard their footsteps overhead, Freda went quickly out into the court-yard, through the great gate, and into the enclosure beyond, waiting for the doctor to come out.

At last the gate opened to let out a youngish-looking man, with a correct professional air of unimpeachable respectability. Freda waited until Mrs. Bean had wished him "good-morning," and shut the gate; then she quickly overtook him, and greeted him with some agitation.

"I beg your pardon, sir," she began modestly; "you have just seen my father, I believe."

"Yes, I have seen him, if Captain Mulgrave was your father."

Freda answered in the affirmative.

"Did you know him?" she then asked.

"I had not that pleasure. You know, Miss Mulgrave, what a secluded life your father always led. I have not been long in Presterby, and although of course, I've heard a great deal about him, I never saw him in life."

"Do you think he shot himself?"

"No, I think not. From the position of the wound I should think it more likely that somebody else shot him."

"And where was the wound?"

"In the back."

There was a pause. Then Freda looked up in the doctor's face.

"They won't tell me anything, so I had to ask you. Thank you for telling me. Good-bye."

She left the doctor, and went back slowly to the gate. Mrs. Bean, who answered her summons, looked angry and disconcerted on learning how she had been employed.

"I think you'd best have followed your own whims and gone back to the convent," she said drily, "we don't want any more questions than necessary asked here just now. There'll be quite enough of a rumpus as it is."

She turned her back upon Freda pretty sharply, and walked back to her kitchen with an offended air. The girl, however, was not to be shaken off.

"Mrs. Bean," she said, following her, "this doctor never saw my father while he was alive!"

There was a pause. Mrs. Bean took up a fork and violently stirred the contents of a saucepan she held.

"Look here, my dear," she said, "what has put all these silly ideas into your head? Don't you know there's going to be an inquest?"

She went on stirring her saucepan without looking up. Freda turned to her eagerly.

"And are these inquest-people men who have known him, and seen him, and talked to him?"

"Why, of course they are. They'll be tradesmen out of the town, most of them, who have supplied him with butter and cheese, beef and candles, for years and years."

"Oh," said Freda, evidently much relieved.

"Now then, you're satisfied, I suppose?" said Mrs. Bean rather curiously.

"Oh, yes, thank you very much."

But in the girl's tone there was still the vestige of a doubt, and she went out with a thoughtful face.

It was a very curious thing, Freda thought, that the servant Blewitt's body should be found shot in the back, and then that her father should be shot in exactly the same way. She puzzled herself over this until her brain reeled, and then she unlocked the front door, and went along the foot-tracks in the snow the whole length of the garden to the wall at the bottom. Here was a door, which she went through, and instead of following the little lane which ran to the right, down towards the town, she still followed the foot-marks over a couple of meadows straight in front of her until, coming to a stone wall, she looked over and discovered the road by which she had come to the Abbey. A great heap of freshly dug up snow stood almost in the middle of the road, and by the help of a shed on the right, Freda was able to identify the spot on which the body of the servant Blewitt had been discovered by Barnabas Ugthorpe.

Freda turned sick with horror. Her mind had jumped, with that splendid feminine inspiration which acts independently of logic, and which is as often marvellously right as stupendously wrong, to the conclusion that the body of Blewitt had been carried into the Abbey. So certain did she feel of this, that the question she asked herself was: Why was this done? And not: Was this done at all? She turned away from the wall, and went back, this time avoiding the foot-track, which she believed to have been made on a guilty errand. She was too horror-struck for tears. She gazed upon the beautiful old house, as she slowly drew near to it again, as she would have done on some unhallowed tomb. The sun, which had been shining brightly all the morning, had begun to melt the snow on the flagged roof, so that patches of moss-grown stone appeared here and there where the white mass had slid down, partially dissolved by the warm rays. The main body of the house was Tudor, of warm red brick with gables, mullioned windows, and stacks of handsome chimneys. But the west wing the so-called Abbot's House, was a plain structure of solid grey stone, with one little scrap of decorated tooth work to bear witness to its connection with the Abbey.

There were secrets behind warm red bricks and venerable grey stone that it was better not to think upon. For the awful conviction was pressing in upon her that if the body of the murdered manservant had been brought there, it could only be to conceal the fact of his murder. Unless, then, it was this mysterious father of hers who had fired the shot, who could it have been?

CHAPTER XII.

THE following was the day of the inquest. It was to be held at the Abbey itself, and Mrs. Bean had swept the drawing-room, and uncovered the furniture in that dismal and damp apartment, so that the coroner and jury might hold their deliberation there. Freda, who followed the housekeeper about like her shadow, without acknowledging that it was because a horror had grown upon her of being left alone in that dreary old house, was helping to dust the old-fashioned ornaments.

"Mrs. Bean," she said at last, stopping in the act of dusting the glass shade over an alabaster urn, in order to clap her hands together to warm them, "aren't you going to light a fire here?"

"Yes, I will presently," answered the housekeeper, whose lips and nose and hands were purple and stiff with cold.

"It will take a long time to warm this great room, won't it?"

"Oh, the fire will soon burn up when it's once lighted."

However, it didn't get lighted at all until half an hour before the coroner and jurymen arrived; and when Mrs. Bean did remember it, she put in the grate a small handful of newspaper and a few damp sticks which gave forth smoke instead of heat, and after hissing and spluttering for some minutes, finally gave up the task of burning altogether.

Freda stood by the kitchen fire, trying to puzzle out the meaning of these strange actions, while Mrs. Bean went out into the court-yard at the summons of the gate-bell. When the housekeeper returned, she met a gaze from the young girl's eyes which made her feel uneasy.

"Are they all come?" asked Freda.

"Yes, the coroner and all of them. They're in the drawing-room now."

"What are they doing now?"

"First, the coroner will charge them; then the witnesses will be examined——"

"What witnesses?" asked Freda quickly.

"Why, Crispin and I."

"Crispin will be examined?"

"Yes," said Nell sharply, "and so will you, if you don't keep out of the way. You'd better go upstairs to your room till they're out of the house. They won't be more than an hour, I should think, at the outside. I'll come up and tell you when they're gone."

So the girl went slowly out of the room, and across the hall, where she could hear the deliberate tones of the coroner charging the jury, and upstairs. But on the landing she stopped, and peeping about to see that she was not watched, she tried the door of her father's room, found that it was locked, and dropping softly on her knees, looked through the key-hole. The bed was opposite to the door.

The body was no longer there.

Freda sprang up from her knees with a white face, ran through the picture-gallery, and shut herself up in her own room. She knew very well that a dead body was not easily moved; half-an-hour ago she had seen it lying on the bed; Mrs. Bean had not been upstairs since; if Crispin was about the house still, could he move such a weight by himself, and carry it down the stairs and out of the house without her having heard or seen him? She sat on a chair near her window, with her head between her hands, trying to puzzle out the meaning of these strange occurrences, until the thought came into her mind that she might perhaps be able, by secreting herself somewhere on the landing outside her father's room, to see the jurymen come up on their investigations, and to hear what they said. So she came softly out of the room, and through the picture-gallery, and out on to the wide landing.

The most desolate spot in the whole house this had always appeared to Freda. As large as a good-sized room, panelled from oaken floor to moulded ceiling with a raised recess by the mullioned window, this might have been made a comfortable as well as handsome corner, while now it was left to the dust and the rats. So thick was the dust on the boards that two paths might be traced in it, the one leading to Captain Mulgrave's room, the other to the door of the picture-gallery. Except on these two tracks the dust lay thick, showing the state of neglect into which the old house had fallen. Freda had often been struck by this, and had even resolved to steal a broom from Mrs. Bean's quarters, and make up herself for the housekeeper's lack either of time or of care.

As her glance wandered over the floor as usual this morning, Freda, therefore, noticed at once that there was a little difference in its appearance. From her father's door there was a semi-circular sweep in the dust towards a little recess on the other side of the head of the staircase. It looked as if something about two feet wide had been dragged along the floor. With a loudly beating heart, Freda followed this track, and reaching the recess, found it to be deeper than she thought, and quite dark; venturing into it, she found that the boards rattled under her feet.

At that moment she heard a door open downstairs, and the hum of several voices, followed by the sound of men's footsteps crossing the hall and ascending the staircase. The coroner and jurymen! She could hear some of the remarks they made to each other in low tones as they came up the stairs, and she found out, by hearing several questions addressed to Crispin, that he was among them. She caught fragments of a good many questions asked about the Captain's habits and the exact position in which the body had been found lying; she heard complaints of the cold and an inquiry why the body had been taken out of the room. Crispin's answers were all given in such a low voice that she could not catch a word of them, but she made out that they satisfied his interrogators. This part of the business occupied only a very few minutes, and then they all tramped out and went downstairs again, the one subject which seemed chiefly to occupy the thoughts of all being the cold, the bitter cold. Their teeth seemed to chatter as they talked. Freda, venturing out of her hiding-place, and passing again over the rattling boards, leaned over the balustrade at the head of the staircase, and saw Mrs. Bean talking in a respectful manner to the coroner. He was complaining of having to go out in the snow to the out-house to view the body.

"Indeed, sir," said the housekeeper, who seemed to Freda to be very nervous and excited, "I am very sorry that I had my poor master's body moved at all; Crispin and I thought it would be more convenient for you, for my poor master's room is, as you saw, so dreadfully crowded up with his furniture and things."

"Oh," returned the coroner, "I'm not blaming you. Of course you did it for the best. We have the doctor's certificate, the viewing the body is merely formal, it will only take a few moments."

He left her and went out by the front door, following the last two jurymen. Freda could not see the door from where she stood, but she heard it close; and she saw the housekeeper, as soon as she was left quite alone, burst into tears and wring her hands desperately.

"It will be found out, it will be found out!" she moaned.

And still sobbing and drying her eyes upon her apron, Mrs. Bean hurried back to her own quarters.

Freda's first impulse was to run after her; but recollecting that the housekeeper was now more likely than ever to be reticent, she refrained, and remaining where she was, awaited the return of the coroner and jurymen in a state of the wildest excitement.

At last she heard the distant sound of voices, and then she heard Mrs. Bean set ajar the kitchen door to listen. Louder and nearer the voices came, and then the foremost man opened the front door and tramped in, followed by the rest.

What had happened? Nothing, apparently, for again the uppermost thought with the men was the intense cold. They were clapping their hands, blowing on their fingers, stamping their feet.

"Like an icehouse, that place!" muttered one.

"They could keep the body there all the winter!" said another.

"Ah couldn't hardly feel ma feet!" added a third.

In the meantime the housekeeper had come out, and greeted them with outward composure, which astonished Freda and excited her admiration.

"Well, gentlemen, and the verdict I suppose is——"

Somebody interrupted her.

"Hush, hush, my good woman. We haven't got so far as that yet. You shall hear all in good time."

The housekeeper apologised, and the coroner and jurymen returned to the drawing-room. In a very few minutes they issued forth again, drawing their mufflers more closely round their necks, and putting on their hats.

Verdict? Oh, yes, the verdict. It was: That the deceased died from the effects of a gunshot wound; but by whose hand the weapon was discharged there was no evidence to show.

Mrs. Bean ushered them out with a decently grave and sad visage. But when she re-entered the house from the court-yard she was singing like a lark.

Freda was puzzled. Back to the recess she went, and feeling with her feet and her crutch very carefully, she soon touched the rattling boards. Then she dropped upon her knees, lit her candle and passed her hand over the floor. Two of the boards were loose, she found, and looking round for something with which to try to raise them, she saw a flattened iron bar lying close under the wall. Suspecting that this had been used previously for the same purpose, she proceeded to raise one of the boards with it. This task easily accomplished, she shifted the board so as to be able to see underneath it.

Extending to a depth of four feet below the surface of the floor, was one of those mysterious enclosures between the ceiling of one room and the floor of the one above, which so often exists in very old houses to testify to forgotten dangers of persecution and pursuit. It was dark, close, musty. Freda bent lower and lower, her eyes fixed in horror on an object at the bottom. Something long, swathed in white: the body of a dead man.

Freda had begun this search full of suspicion; but the shock was almost as great as if she had been entirely unprepared for the discovery of this ghastly secret. She did not scream, although after the first shock she put her hands before her mouth in the belief that she had done so. She felt benumbed, stunned. Who was it? She must look, she must find out, if the discovery killed her. With trembling hands she picked up her candle, which had fallen and gone out, and relighting it, peered down at the dead face.

For the first moment she did not recognise it, or death had refined the coarse outline and effaced the sinister expression. Presently, however, came full recollection. It was the dead face of the servant Blewitt.

CHAPTER XIII.

THE body of Blewitt, still wearing its clothes, had been wrapped in a sheet and dragged to this hiding-place that morning. As soon as she recognised the dead face, Freda sprang up from her knees, dropping her candle and forgetting to replace the loose board. With flying feet, not caring now who heard her, she went clattering down the stairs, sick with horror of the house and everything in it, capable of only one thought, one wish: that she could leave it at once, never to enter it again.

The front door into the garden was ajar. Freda ran out into the snow, which was now falling pretty thickly. But the intense cold was pleasant to her: it seemed to give a little relief to her feverishly hot head. She ran to the bottom of the garden; but the door in the wall was locked. Returning slowly, despondently, she caught sight of the door leading to the out-house and stable-yard. This had been left open. She saw the track of many feet leading to one of the out-houses, and guessing that it was that in which the jury had viewed her father's body, she instantly resolved to satisfy herself on one point of the mystery. The door was not locked. Creeping in, her heart beating wildly with excitement, Freda found herself in a bare stone-paved building, which might once have been a court-house. It was badly lighted by a small window, high up in the right-hand wall. Near the middle of the floor was a coffin, supported by trestles. Freda approached slowly, her feet slipping on the pavement, which was wet with snow brought in by many feet. She was so much stupefied by the sensations of the morning that she was no longer able to feel any shock acutely. One dull pang of astonishment rather than any other feeling shot through her as she looked in, expecting to see her father's face.

The coffin was empty.

Freda staggered away out of the building. She was now only capable of one sensation—a longing to escape so strong, so fixed, that it became at once a resolution. She stole past the stables, a long line of stone buildings, with remnants of monastic character in blocked up Gothic doorways and disused niches. No one had passed that way this morning, for the night's snow was untrodden. From the other extremity of the line of stables, however, there were footprints in the snow going backwards and forwards through the stone entrance to the open space in front of the banqueting-hall. From this entrance the gates had been torn down, so that the one barrier between Freda and liberty was now the outer gates at the lodge.

She had nothing to fear from the blind eyes of the blocked-up windows in the roofless hall. So she went across the enclosure to the lodge, and tried the iron gates. They were fastened. She did not dare to summon the woman in charge to open for her: hatless as she was, she would never be allowed to pass. This place, with its secret locks, its well-guarded exits, its high stone walls, was practically a prison at the will of its owners. Her only chance was to wait until the gates were opened for some one else to go in or out, and then to slip past and take her chance of being unnoticed. Of course this plan could not be tried until darkness set in; but it was such a gloomy day that dusk could not fail to be early. In the meantime she must find a hiding-place. There was no nook or corner in this great bare enclosure into which she could creep; she had to retrace her steps, forgetting the tell-tale print of her poor little feet in the snow, to the stable-yard, where she found an unlocked door. Entering a four-stall stable, which had evidently not been used for years except as a storage-place for lumber, she sat down on an empty packing-case, and prepared to wait.

She was so bitterly cold that she began to feel too benumbed to move or even to think. She tried to clap her hands together, but the movement caused her so much pain that she gave up this attempt, and remained in a crouching attitude with her arms folded. The incident of the morning faded from her mind, so that she soon almost forgot how she came there. Perhaps she was dreaming it all. Then she drew herself up with a start, remembering stories that she had heard of the danger of falling asleep in the cold. Danger! why danger? If she died there she would go to heaven, and meet the Mother-Superior and Sister Agnes and the rest some day, and perhaps God would forgive her father for the sake of her prayers. She could pray for him now, die praying for him, that was the best thing she could do. For now, although the mystery was not cleared, there seemed no doubt possible that he was the murderer of the man Blewitt.

So she fell on her knees, and, supporting herself against a pile of old hampers and mouldy straw, tried to pray. But she could not keep her mind from straying, and, with the words of supplication still on her lips, the thought would flit through her mind that it was to Barnabas Ugthorpe she must escape; or again, the figure of Dick Heritage would seem to appear before her eyes, with the good-humoured smile which had so won her heart. And then prayers and thoughts alike merged into a sensation of nameless horror, which she could neither understand nor fight against.

At this point, when she was on the verge of insensibility, there came a noise, a light, a touch. She was shaken by the shoulder, then lifted up bodily, and some one spoke to her in a voice which at first seemed to come from a long way off, and then suddenly, without any warning, sounded close to her ear.

"Wake up, child, wake up. Are you asleep?" Then it was that the change came, and the words almost stunned her like a loud cry: "Merciful God! She is not dead, not dead?"

Freda raised her head feebly.

"Is it you, Barnabas?" she said.

There was no answer, and the girl had time to collect her thoughts. Raising herself, she found she had been supported by the arms of Crispin Bean, who hung over her with a face of dumb solicitude. Struggling away from him, with what would have been a shriek if her vocal powers had been fully restored, she ran towards the door, but stumbled blindly. He ran after her and supported her against her will.

"Let me go, I entreat you let me go," she pleaded hoarsely.

"Presently, perhaps," answered Crispin in a gentle tone, "but I want to talk to you first."

Freda was still too benumbed with cold and fright to offer much resistance. Finding that her hands were blue and stiff and that she looked starved and miserable, Crispin lifted her right off her feet, and, without heeding her weak ejaculations of protest, carried her out of the stable, holding her with her face against his shoulder, so that she could not see. Freda protested and tried to cry out, but he only laughed at her.

"Oh," she cried hoarsely, when she found that Crispin stopped to turn the key in a lock, "don't take me into that dreadful house again; I shall go out of my senses if you do."

"No, you won't."

He spoke rather peremptorily, and she was cowed into silence. The next moment she heard the tramp of his feet on stone flags and heard the echo of every step, so that she fancied they must be passing through a passage or chamber with a vaulted stone roof. In spite of the warnings she had received, she first tried to lift her head and look round, and being checked in this attempt by the wary Crispin, she suddenly endeavoured to jump out of his arms. He laughed grimly.

"Don't you ever intend to learn prudence?" he asked.

Freda was desperate.

"No," she cried with determination. "I don't care what happens to me as long as I have to stay in this wicked place, and if my curiosity causes me to be sent away any sooner, why, I shall be very glad."

"I suppose it depends where you will be sent away to?"

"No. I would rather be anywhere in the world, yes, anywhere than here."

She was now being carried up a flight of wooden steps. She counted twenty. The next flight, a shorter one, was of stone. Then came a few steps of level ground, and again Crispin proceeded to turn a key. When they had passed through this second door, and while Crispin was engaged in relocking it, Freda took the opportunity to drop her own handkerchief unseen by him. Then she was carried on again, along boarded floors and through two or three more doors, down a flight of stairs and to the dining-room. Here Crispin put her down and pushed her gently inside. Then he summoned Mrs. Bean, who looked at her with a puzzled and frightened face, and told her to bring something for the young lady to eat. Freda, who had sunk down in a chair by the fire to warm herself, sprang up at these words, and interrupted Crispin.

"Not for me," she cried. "I will never eat anything again till I'm out of this house."

"Then you'll starve," said Crispin quietly.

The girl flew up, shaking with fear, and horror, and anger. Mrs. Bean, who kept her eyes on the ground, but looked exceedingly troubled, remained in a half-furtive manner near the door.

"Do you think I care?" cried the girl, in a broken voice, "I know this house is a place to murder people in, and if I'm to be hidden away under the floor, like the poor man I found upstairs, I don't care by what way you kill me first!"

The housekeeper's face blanched at the girl's words, but she did not utter a word, did not even look up. Crispin dismissed her with a nod, and turned to the young girl. Freda cowered on a chair, expecting a great outburst of anger from him. But there was a long silence, during which she heard him poke the fire and push the blazing logs together. At last he said, in an unemotional voice:

"I am not surprised that you want to know the meaning of the strange things you have seen and heard here."

Freda answered passionately, only raising her head sufficiently to be heard,

"I do know the meaning of it all. It is you who have murdered both my father and Blewitt!"

"The d——l it is!" exclaimed Crispin, in unmistakable amusement and surprise. "If you give information against me on that ground, you will create a small sensation in Presterby."

Freda perceived at once that her shot was wide of the mark. She sat up and looked at him.

"Well, if you didn't, then who did?"

Crispin looked at her steadily, with rather a comical expression, for a long time. Then he shook his head.

"Of course you won't believe me," he said; "but I don't know."

"But wasn't it you that brought Blewitt's body into the house?"

Crispin nodded.

"And had it seen by the doctor?"

"Yes."

"And then hid it under the floor?"

"Well, I had a hand in that too."

"Why?"

"Because, if the body had been found in the road, your father would have been hanged for the murder."

"But he didn't do it, he didn't do it," wailed Freda, in a tone which implored him to agree with her.

"Perhaps he thought a live man could prove his own innocence better than a dead one," suggested Crispin drily.

Freda sprang up, and in great excitement, forgetting her crutch, half hobbled, half leapt across the room until she stood close to him, face to face, eye to eye.

She seized his hands, and devoured his face with eyes which seemed to burn and shoot forth flames.

"Then he is—not—dead?" she hissed out, with hot breath.

"Hush, hush, for goodness' sake, girl, hold your tongue," said Crispin, whose turn it was to feel alarmed. "Do you know, you little fool, what it would mean to everybody in this house if such—such craziness were suspected?"

"Oh, yes," said she, turning suddenly grave, "of course I know that. Tell me, Crispin, where is he? where is my father?"

"He's where he hasn't got to trust his life to your prattling tongue," said Crispin gruffly.

"He is about the house somewhere, I expect," said Freda yearningly. "I saw the empty coffin," she continued, in a whisper of suppressed horror, "not more than half an hour after they had all gone, so I am sure he cannot have got far. He is in hiding somewhere about. Oh, Crispin, Crispin, you are in all the secret, you were the chief witness, you helped in it all, you *do* know. Tell me, tell me where he is. Is he going away? Can't I see him, just for one moment. I would not say one word."

She seemed to be moving him: as she clung about him, he turned away his head uneasily. She continued her pleading, more and more earnestly, more and more passionately, until at last he burst out: "He was a bad man. You'd better forget him."

"How can he be so bad when you and your wife take all sorts of risks to shield him?"

"It's to our interest."

"I believe you're a better man than you pretend, Crispin," said Freda after a pause.

"Perhaps so. Here's your tea," he answered laconically, as Mrs. Bean, tray in hand, entered the room.

CHAPTER XIV.

THE funeral was to take place on the following day. It was not without a shudder that Freda made her way up to her bedroom that night, although she had taken the precaution of insisting that Mrs. Bean should accompany her to the very door. Even then she was reluctant to let the housekeeper go.

"Mrs. Bean," she said in a whisper, as she clung to the housekeeper's rough arms after bidding her good-night. "What room is there under this one?"

The housekeeper looked rather uneasy, and laughed.

"Really, I don't know what it was. It's a long time since any of the rooms in this wing have been used except this one."

"But it was used the other night! I heard men talking there. Crispin said they were the sailors of my father's yacht."

"Well, if he said that, what more do you want to know?"

"I want to know how they got in. I haven't seen any door on the outside of this part of the house."

"I suppose they came through the other part then."

"I suppose so."

There was a pause, and Mrs. Bean shuffled a step nearer the door. Then she turned, to whisper plaintively:

"Child, I wish you'd be persuaded to keep a still tongue in your head."

But not only was Freda unable to obey this precept, she was further resolved to use both eyes and ears on her own account. Being assured now that both Crispin and Nell were her friends, she felt bold enough to try to satisfy herself on the one point of greatest interest to her: Was her father still in the house? Perhaps that very night he was going away, under cover of the darkness! Stung to action by this suggestion, conquering even the horror of the day's adventures, she took her candle from the table and went out of the room into the stone passage. Freda softly open the door into the gallery, and shielding her candle with her hand, to minimise the risk of its light betraying her, crept along that portion of it which ran along the west side of the house. As she went she caught sight of something white on the ground, close underneath the panelling. It was the handkerchief she had slyly dropped that day, in the hope that it would afford some clue to the way Crispin was bringing her.

A close inspection of the panelling disclosed a tiny keyhole in the ornamental part of the carving, and although the panel in which it was pierced fitted perfectly into its place, yet a tap revealed the fact that there was a hollow or open space behind. She hailed this discovery with much excitement. This then was a very good place to watch, if her father really

66

was in hiding about the house. The question now was how to conceal herself. There was nothing in the gallery but pictures, and a row of chairs. As she stood debating with herself, she heard footsteps, as it seemed to her, behind the panelling. In a frenzy of excitement she instantly blew out her candle, and scurried across the gallery to the furthest corner, where she crouched in a heap on the floor. She had not to wait long. A little scraping sound, and a panelled door opened from the other side. Then Freda heard a distant murmur of voices, and the next moment the man who had opened the door stepped into the gallery.

Freda need not have been afraid of discovery. The man carried no light, and she could only dimly see the outline of his figure as he crossed the floor noiselessly towards one of the long windows. This he pushed up with only the very faintest sound, and putting his head out, said in a low voice:

"Ready?"

Freda who in her eagerness to discover whether this was her father on the point of escaping, had crawled along the bare boards close under the windows, was listening, watching with her heart beating so violently that she was afraid it would betray her. She heard no answer given, but the man drew in his head and retired again through the panel-door. By his gait she knew that he was not a gentleman, and therefore that he could not be her father. She heard him go down the stone steps, which she guessed to be those up which Crispin had carried her; and then making the most of her opportunity, she ran to the open window, and looked out.

A man was waiting in the court-yard underneath. He must have heard her footsteps, for he raised his head, and seeing that somebody was at the window, he said, in a hoarse whisper:

"Eh, but thou'rt a long toime to-neght. Thou'rt not very spry for a sailor! Art droonk again?"

Freda drew in her head before he had time to see that it was a woman whom he was addressing; but not before she had seen enough of his figure, and heard enough of his rough, thick voice, to ask herself whether this was not Josiah Kemm, of the "Barley Mow." The man, whoever he was, had hardly finished speaking, when from behind the panelling she heard again the distant murmur of voices, and footsteps coming up the stone staircase. She hastily retreated from the window, not to the corner she had left, but to the door by which she had entered the gallery. She had scarcely done so when the man she had previously seen reappeared. As she was now much nearer to him, she could distinctly see that he had upon his back a package about three feet square which was evidently heavy. This he carried across to the window, and let down by means of a rope into the court-yard. Then she heard faintly the voice of the man in the court-

67

yard asking some question. Although she could not distinguish his words, the answer of the man above, "No. Nobody," told her that the question had concerned her own appearance at the window. Judging therefore that an investigation might follow, she crept along the stone passage and locked herself in her own room as quickly as she could.

Next morning, however, she would not have her breakfast until she had found an opportunity of exchanging a few words with Crispin Bean.

"Crispin," she began solemnly, "you remember telling me that the sailors of my father's yacht were in the house one night when I heard a noise?"

He grunted an affirmative rather shortly.

"Well," she went on, "they were here again last night."

"What of that?" said Crispin.

"I believe they were stealing something. I saw one of them throw a package out of the window to a man in the court-yard underneath."

"I should like to know what you don't see," grumbled Crispin, not very well pleased.

Freda drew herself up.

"I ought to know all that goes on in my own house," said she, holding her head back with a pretty little air. "And I mean to go over the place, and see that there is no way for people to get in that have no business here. And as for this yacht, it is of no use now, so what is the use of paying a lot of sailors for doing nothing."

Crispin looked down on the floor, with rather a whimsical expression of face.

"They're all old servants of your father's, you know. If they're turned off, they're very likely to starve. As for what you thought was stealing, it was only an old salt, who has been one of the yacht's crew for seven years, throwing down his own traps to a friend from the town who had promised to take care of them."

"But why did he do it so mysteriously, and at night?" asked Freda, still incredulous.

But Crispin was tired of answering her questions, or else he had no reply to give, for without any more words he proceeded to light his pipe and walk away.

CHAPTER XV.

THE day of the funeral was a trying one for Freda. She ran up to her own room when the undertaker's men arrived, and would have remained there for hours if she had not been disturbed by a peremptory knock at her door, and by Crispin's voice telling her to get ready to go to the church. She opened the door, trembling with fear and repugnance.

"Crispin," she entreated, "don't make me go! I can't go, when I know it is only a sham. I can't pretend to be sorry, I can't, and I won't."

"Oh, well, nobody will expect much sorrow from you, but you will have to go to the church. Haven't you got a black dress?"

"Yes."

"Well, put it on, and make haste. Nell is waiting."

"Aren't you going?"

For Crispin wore his usual costume: a threadbare velveteen coat, evidently one of his late master's, riding-breeches and gaiters.

He shook his head.

"No, I can't stand old Staynes. If I went I should laugh."

"People won't think it very respectful of you, will they?"

"People know me. Besides, I don't care what they think. Now you look sharp."

He went away, and Freda very reluctantly obeyed his injunctions, dressed herself all in black and went downstairs to the hall, where she found Nell waiting for her.

"Come along," said the housekeeper rather crossly.

And seizing Freda by the arm, she dashed across the court-yard and the enclosure beyond, and dragged her through the open iron gates, outside which the funeral procession could be seen on its way through the churchyard. Freda felt so sick with disgust at the part she had to play in the farce, that she looked unutterably miserable, and heard sympathetic murmurs from many lips, as Nell with a strong hand half dragged her through the crowd.

"Poor little thing!" "Doan't she look unhappy, poor lass!" and many such exclamations reached Freda's ears and made her furious. Nell seemed to feel that there was a danger of the girl's wrathful honesty breaking out, for she hurried her on into the church, and heaved a sigh of relief when she had pushed the girl into a square pew lined with green baize, immediately over which an old-fashioned three-decker pulpit frowned. Freda, at last distracted from her thoughts of the proceedings, looked about her in amazement.

"Is this a *church*?" she whispered.

Her ignorance was pardonable. Surely never yet did wild churchwardens in the frenzy of their Puritanism so run riot in a church before. Originally a plain Norman structure, erected by the monks of Presterby Abbey, and given to the townsfolk when their own Abbey church was completed, it had been transformed by later improvements into a very good copy of the interior of a ship. Clumsy little galleries had been erected wherever there was room for one, even before the old Norman chancel-arch. These galleries were entered from the outside of the church by covered flights of wooden steps, made on the model of the entrance to a bathing-machine. The roof was perforated by small cabin windows; the whole of the interior was covered with white-wash, including any small fragments of stone-work which the modern improvements had left visible; the Norman windows had all been carefully stopped up, and replaced by ordinary house windows, filled with small panes of poor glass. The only decorations were an enormous coloured coat of arms over the gallery of the chancel-arch, and a series of texts, indifferently spelt and painted coarsely on square wooden boards, which hung on the white-washed walls.

Nell scented popery in the girl's innocent question, and answered with a frown.

"Of course it is. People don't want tawdry fal-lals to help them to worship God, when they come in the right spirit," she said severely. "Be quiet, here comes the Vicar."

She thrust a prayer-book into the hand of the girl, who did not, however, follow the service, and who certainly could not understand much from the mumbling delivery of Mr. Staynes. She was shocked at the deception which was being carried out through all these solemn details, and when she was led to the side of the grave she shuddered and looked away.

When it was all over, Nell tried hard to lead her at once back to the house. But little Mrs. Staynes was too quick for her. Trotting up to the girl with what was only a decorous caricature of grief on her round apple face, she said:

"You must bear up, my dear Miss Mulgrave. 'Whom the Lord loveth He chasteneth.' We must be resigned to His will. You must control your grief, my dear."

"I haven't any grief," said Freda in spite of Nell's warning fingers on her arm.

Poor little Mrs. Staynes looked shocked and disconcerted.

"Of course, my dear, we know it's not the same as if you had been brought up at home. Indeed, I told the poor Captain so, times without number, but he hardened his heart and would not listen to me. But still, of course, you feel all that it is right for a daughter to feel under the circumstances."

Mrs. Staynes was getting hurried and nervous. Indeed, she could only give half her mind to the consolation of her husband's bereaved young parishioner, for she held the Vicar's goloshes in her hand, and if she did not turn up with them exactly at the moment when he was ready to put them on, both he and she were apt to think that she had only escaped perdition by the skin of her teeth.

Before Freda had time to answer, a rather loud and peremptory voice close to them startled both ladies. Standing beside them was a robust-looking man in a close cap and thick travelling ulster, who suddenly struck in:

"And pray what is it, ma'am, that a daughter should feel under the circumstances of losing a father who had, from a sentimental point of view no claim to the name?"

He took Freda's hand and shook it warmly, almost before she had had time to recognise in him her friend of the journey.

"A friend of yours, Miss Mulgrave?" asked the Vicar's wife rather primly.

The new-comer replied for her.

"Yes, ma'am, a friend of Miss Mulgrave's—whether she likes it or not," said he.

"This gentleman has been very, very kind to me," said Freda, recovering her voice. "On the journey here I——"

"Was indebted to this good gentleman for a biscuit and a cup of tea," chimed in the stranger's good-humoured voice. "And unlike most ladies to whom one may chance to render a small service of the kind, she remembers it."

"It is not always prudent for young ladies to make chance friends on the railway," said Mrs. Staynes.

"It is convenient though, madam, in case of an accident. And perhaps the young lady had the judgment to see that there's very little of the gay Lothario about me."

"Oh, certainly," said Mrs. Staynes, who thought the stranger rather flippant. "Ah, there's the Vicar. I—er—I—— *Good*-morning, Miss Mulgrave."

With a curious little salutation to the stranger, which was half a bow and half a "charity bob," the Vicar's wife trotted off, waving the goloshes. Nell whispered to Freda to make haste home. The girl withdrew her arm suddenly.

"You go home, Mrs. Bean," she said. "I will come in a few minutes."

Then she turned, in spite of Nell's remonstrances and rejoined the stranger.

The crowds of poor-looking people who had collected to see the funeral had begun very slowly to melt away, and Freda overheard enough of the remarks they exchanged to learn that her father had been very good to the poor, especially to the seafaring folk, and that there was much genuine sorrow at his death. She wanted to speak to some of these people, to assure them that as far as lay in her power, she would fill his place to them. But she was too shy. Her friend had to speak to her to recall her attention to himself.

"Rum business this altogether," he said. "They say your father was found dead in his room, don't they?"

"Yes," mumbled Freda, with white lips.

"Nothing said about his being shot out-of-doors, eh?"

She shook her head.

"No man accused of having murdered him?"

"No."

"Well, I could tell a tale—only it wouldn't do for me just now to be telling tales, and bringing myself into prominence. Besides, without corroboration, I daresay my tale wouldn't amount to much. Still——"

"Don't, don't," said Freda hoarsely, "don't find out anything, don't try to. What good could it do now?"

He looked at her searchingly, not unkindly. Yet there was something in the expression of his face which impressed Freda with the belief that he was a man with whom no prayers, no entreaties would avail anything when he had once made up his mind.

She went on, as if anxious to change the subject: "You stayed the night with Barnabas, didn't you?"

"Yes, and came on the next day, and climbed up to this old place because I wanted to see where you were going to live."

"Did you meet anybody?"

"Only one person, a rough-looking fellow, who told me I was trespassing, and ordered me into the road. I had got over into the fields between the house and the ruin."

"Was he tall, with a short greyish beard?"

"Yes."

"That was Crispin Bean."

"Oh, yes, I've heard of him; he was a devoted servant to your father. I've been making inquiries to find out whose care you'd been left in."

"That was very kind of you. Then you've been in Presterby on business? What business?"

"Ah, that's the question."

"Secret business then?"

"No wise man cares to have his business prattled about."

"But you will tell me if I guess right?"

"Perhaps I'll go as far as that."

"And you will tell me your name?"

"John Thurley."

"And where you come from?"

"London."

"John Thurley, of London." She meditated a moment. "You have come on some business connected with trade?"

"Well, not exactly," said he, as if rather offended at the suggestion.

"I mean Free Trade," corrected Freda.

John Thurley was perceptibly startled. He paused for a few moments, looking at her attentively, before he asked, in an altered tone:

"What do you know about that?"

"Oh, I've heard people talking about it—on the journey. Nobody seems to think it beneath him to be interested in trade up here."

"You mean Free Trade?"

"Yes."

"And I suppose you don't know that Free Trade means smuggling?"

Now Freda had had suspicions of this before, so that she was not greatly surprised by the information. She jumped at once to a conclusion suggested by it.

"You are up here to look after the smugglers then?"

"Well, I'm not much given to disguise of any sort," he admitted bluntly, "but the feeling up here is so strongly against the law and with the evildoers, that a little caution is absolutely necessary."

"Have you caught them yet?" asked Freda with curiosity.

"No. Everybody seems banded together in a league to help them."

"How are you sure there are any?"

"Well, we've had suspicions for years of a great organisation for smuggling, admirably planned and carried out, defrauding the revenue to the extent of thousands of pounds annually. The plans of these wretches were so well laid that, though we have again and again caught the receivers of smuggled spirits and tobacco, we have never yet been able to lay hands upon the big offenders, and it is only lately that we have had information pointing to the Yorkshire coast as the probable centre of the trade. I have been sent down to investigate."

"And what will be done to these men if they are caught?"

"Well, the usual punishment for smuggling is by fines; to be strictly correct it is the value of the article smuggled and three times the duty on it. But if, as we suspect, we get hold of a chief or chiefs of a regular gang, why, then, he or they, whichever it proves to be, will have to be proceeded against by some method more convincing."

"Oh, yes," said Freda.

"I am going southward for a few days, to visit two or three places further down the coast. When I come back I shall call at the Abbey to see you: will you make me welcome for an hour?"

"Indeed I would if I might, if I could," said she mournfully. "But I don't feel that I am the real mistress there; there are Crispin and his wife."

Her friend frowned and spoke with kindly impatience.

"I can't bear to think of your having to put up with the companionship and protection of those people! I shall find out your guardian—you must have some guardian, and get him to send you back to the convent, at least for a little while, since that seems to be your ideal of happiness."

"My ideal of happiness!" echoed Freda wonderingly.

"Yes, you said so the other day at the 'Barley Mow.'"

"Did I!" said the girl, blushing.

"Yes, you did. Now, I suppose, it is something else."

She hung her head.

"Some young fellow has been talking to you!"

Freda gave him a glance of terror. How horribly shrewd he was, to touch at once upon a kind of secret she hardly knew herself yet! She would admit nothing, yet she was afraid to be silent. He might blunder upon some other sensitive truth if she did not speak. So she evaded the point.

"You seem here in England," she began proudly, "to think that there is only one subject which can interest a girl!"

"Quite true. Everywhere else it is the same. There *is* only one. I don't want to force your confidence, but I know that you stayed at Oldcastle Farm on the night of the journey."

It seemed to Freda that an expression of disappointment crossed Mr. Thurley's face when she made no answer to this, and the next moment he seemed suddenly in a great hurry to be off. Shaking her hand heartily in both his, he uttered a number of good wishes, and questions about her welfare with a bluff sincerity of interest which touched her. She watched him as he went down the steep churchyard without one look behind him, and the tears came into her eyes as she felt that here was a friend, none the less real for being a new acquaintance, going away.

Freda felt almost like a prisoner coming of his own accord back to the confinement from which he had escaped, as she pulled the lodge-bell and passed through the iron gates. Mrs. Bean, who was probably on the lookout, heard the loud clang, and was ready to open the inner gate. She did not seem in very good humour.

"You have been a long time talking with your gentleman friend," she said coldly. "I didn't know those were convent manners, to encourage every man who chooses to cast sheep's-eyes at one!"

Poor Freda entered the dining-room thoroughly heart-sick and disgusted. Why did they say those coarse things to her, and about people she liked too! She felt so miserable that, instead of trying to eat, she sat down on the hearth-rug and cried, with her head on a chair.

Presently Crispin looked in at the window, and coming round to the door of the room, opened it and peeped in.

"What's the matter?" asked he.

Freda sprang from the floor, but refused to give any other explanation than that she was tired, and had stood talking in the churchyard.

"Talking! Who to?"

"To the gentleman who was kind to me in the train. Mrs. Bean, doesn't seem to think it was right of me to talk to him; but he was very kind."

Crispin said nothing to this, but persuaded her to eat her dinner, waiting upon her himself. When she had finished, and he was making up the fire for her, she suddenly addressed him.

"Crispin," she said, "I want to ask you a question. There is a thing which some people call Free Trade, and other people call smuggling. Which do you call it?"

Crispin, who was holding the poker in his hand, stopped short in his work, and remained for a few seconds quite still, without looking at her. Then he answered in a very quiet manner, and went on making up the fire.

"Smuggling, of course. And, what did your friend of the journey call it?"

He suddenly turned as he spoke, and under the piercing gaze which he directed upon her, Freda fancied that all her little girlish fancies and secrets were laid bare to his eyes.

"He called it smuggling too," she answered.

"And what was his name?"

Freda hesitated. Such a hard, disagreeable tone seemed suddenly to be heard in Crispin's voice. He repeated the question.

"His name is John Thurley."

Without asking her any more questions, seeming, in fact, to become suddenly unconscious of her presence, Crispin abruptly left her to herself.

CHAPTER XVI.

FREDA MULGRAVE had come face to face with the most difficult problem of conduct she had ever encountered. There was now no shirking the fact that her father was the organiser and head of a band of men who carried on smuggling in a systematic and determined manner. It was evident too that, if occasion came, they were quite as ready for still guiltier exploits as their fore-runners of a by-gone time. Whether, as she feared with a sickly horror, it was her father who had shot Blewitt, or whether the servant had been murdered by some one else, it was clear that his death was connected with the nefarious enterprises in which the whole country-side seemed to be so deeply engaged. She passed a miserable night, awake for a great part of the time, fancying she heard in the many night-noises of the old house, voices and footsteps, cries and even blows.

Next morning she wrote a long letter to Sister Agnes, saying that she had been left alone in a position of great difficulty, and asking for the prayers of all her old friends at the convent that she might do what was right.

Mrs. Bean, who came in while she was directing the envelope, offered to take it to the post, and Freda, with a reluctance of which she felt ashamed, gave it into her keeping.

Then for ten days the poor child lived on the daily hope and expectation of an answer.

During all that time she never once saw Crispin, and although she two or three times tried to break through the ice of Nell's reticence, she always failed. For blank, deaf, impervious stolidity, and an ignorance of everything outside her kitchen which approached the admirable, Nell could never have had an equal. Crispin was away on business. This was the most Freda could learn from her.

So the dull days passed, the wished-for letter never coming. For the first two days the snow remained thick on the ground, and when it began to melt the roads were in such a bad state that it was still impossible for Freda to go out. Nell unlocked the library and made a fire there. And in this old room, with its quaintly moulded ceiling, its rows upon rows of musty-smelling books, its dust and its cobwebs, the young girl passed her time, diving for the most part in records of the county, of ancient priory and dismantled castle. Her flesh would creep and her breath come fast as she read of lawless deeds in the time past, and thought that even while she read, acts just as illegal, if not as daring, might be taking place under the very roof which sheltered her.

At the end of the ten days, however, it seemed to Freda one morning that the patches of green on the snow-covered fields had grown much wider; and she said, first to herself and then to Nell, that the roads, if not yet clear, must now be passable to and from the town. Mrs. Bean looked at her out of the corners of her eyes.

"What you, coming from a walled-up convent, can want with walks, is more than I can understand. However, you can go over the ruins if you like."

And Nell unlocked a side-door in the wall of the garden which admitted her into the meadow in which the Abbey-church stood.

"You'll be safe there," said Nell, half to herself, as Freda passed through. "You can't do any worse harm than getting your feet wet, and that's your own fault."

"Safe! Of course I shall be safe!" laughed Freda.

But it occurred to her, as she turned and noted Nell's furtive glance at her, that it was not with her personal safety that the housekeeper was concerned.

Freda cared little for this; she was half-crazy with the joy of being again by herself in the open air; and the ruins of the old church, as they rose above her in their worn majesty against the morning sky, filled her with delight and awe. She was approaching the old pile from the southwest, the quarter in which least of the building remained. Scarcely a trace was left of the south aisle or the south transept. Between the ruined west front and the pillars on the south side of the choir there was nothing left but grass-grown mounds of fallen masonry and one solitary pillar, massive and erect as when, seven hundred years ago, pious hands placed the stones which were to defy, through long centuries, the biting sea air, the keen north wind, the storms which beat upon the cliffs, and the waves which, decade by decade, had sapped and swallowed up, bit by bit, the once fertile Abbey lands. Nearer to the cliff's edge now than in its prime, the dismantled church still filled one of its old offices, and formed, with its lofty choir and mouldering pinnacles, a landmark from the sea.

Freda began to cry as she stole reverently into the roofless choir. She had had no opportunity, in her secluded life, of visiting ruins as showplaces; to her this was still a church, as holy as when the monks kept watch before the altar. A sentiment of peace entered into her for the first time since her arrival in England as she wandered about, not heeding the fall of melting snow on her head and shoulders, and listened to the shriek of the sea-birds as they wheeled in the air above. She thought she had never seen anything so beautiful as the graceful succession of pointed arches, with their clustered shafts, and the triforium above, with the long-hidden beauties of its carving now exposed to the light of day. Time had mellowed the tint of the walls to a soft grey, deepening here and there into red. Crowned kings, winged angels, stern-faced saints still looked out to sea from the north side, with eager necks outstretched, all the deep meaning the old monkish sculptors knew how to express in stone still to be discerned in their weatherworn outlines. The gulls perched upon them; in summer the wallflowers grew about them; but still they kept watch and ward until, one by one, by storm and stress of weather they were loosened in their places, and fell, sentinels who had done their work, into the long grass underneath.

The north transept was still almost entire. An arcade ran round the lower part of the wall, and in one of the arches was an old pointed wooden door, leading by a circular staircase of steep steps, to the passages in the walls above. This door was locked. Yet it must still be used, thought Freda. For she noticed that the grass was worn away before it, and that a narrow track had been beaten thence as far as one of the windows on the north side of the nave. Here a gap had evidently been intentionally made in the stone, and looking through, Freda perceived that the foot-track went through the meadow outside as far as the stone wall which bordered the road.

As she was looking at this path, she caught sight of two young men on horseback whom, little as she could see of them above the stone wall, she at once recognised. They were Robert and Richard Heritage. Both saw her, raised their hats, and reined in their horses.

Freda pretended not to see them, yet she was conscious of a great uplifting of the heart when they dismounted, tied their horses up in the yard of a dismantled cottage at the other side of the road, and climbing over the stone wall with the agility of cats, came along the foot-path towards her.

"They have used that foot-path before," thought Freda.

CHAPTER XVII.

To Freda's perhaps rather prejudiced mind, the contrast between the two cousins seemed even stronger than when she had seen them a fortnight before at their own home. The fact that both were evidently harassed and anxious only emphasised the difference between them; for while Robert looked savage and sullen even under the smile with which he approached her, Dick seemed to Freda's shy eyes to look haggard, downcast and depressed to an extent which sent a pang through her heart.

Robert came first, cracking his riding-whip and singing, and assuming a jauntiness belied by the expression of his face. He raised his hat again as he came through the ruined window, and greeted Freda with much deference. He made a feint of holding out his hand, but the young lady took no notice of it.

"I am afraid," began he, in a deprecating tone, "that our acquaintance did not begin in the most auspicious possible manner, Miss Mulgrave."

"No, and I did not expect to see you again."

Freda was far too unsophisticated to be otherwise than cruelly direct of speech. Robert Heritage, however, was not easily disconcerted.

"But if the reason of my daring to appear before you again is to make my peace in the humblest manner?"

"There is no need to be humble to me. You said so the last time I saw you."

"Pray forget everything I said then, and let us begin afresh. I had had a good deal of worry that day, and I spoke to you under a misapprehension."

"I would rather have you remain under it, and not speak to me again."

"You are very unforgiving."

Freda hung her head. They used to tell her that at the convent. It was true too, she felt. She had never been able to humble herself to docile obedience—to the doctrine of forgiveness of enemies. Nothing could be wrong in those she loved, nothing right in those she did not love. And she did not love Robert Heritage. Guiltily, therefore, she said, after a minute's pause:

"I will hear what you have to say."

Robert made a grimace to his cousin, to imply that this insignificant little girl was giving herself great airs. As for Dick, Freda had steadily avoided meeting his eyes, and he stood in the background, silently watching the flying sea-mews, without taking any active part in this interview.

"In the first place," said Robert, still with a great show of deference, "I came—my cousin and I came, to express our regrets at your sad bereavement, at your father's death, in fact."

He looked at her rather curiously. Freda blushed.

"Thank you," she said hurriedly.

"Yes," he went on slowly, "we were very much shocked to hear about it, and very much surprised too. For I was just coming over here to inquire if Captain Mulgrave could tell me what had become of a servant of mine, a man you saw at our house, Miss Mulgrave; Blewitt, I dare say you remember him?"

"Yes, I do," answered Freda, who had grown very pale.

"I sent him over here with a letter, a message to your father. From that day to this he has never been seen, and we have been unable to get any tidings of him. In the meantime comes the news of Captain Mulgrave's having committed suicide. Under the circumstances, your father being known as a violent man, and the message being an unwelcome one, it was impossible to help thinking that the two events might have some connection with each other."

"Well," said Freda slowly, "but as both Blewitt and my father are—gone, I don't see how the truth is ever to be found now; unless, indeed, the person who knows most about it should confess."

Robert's face flushed a little.

"I am afraid it will be difficult to clear your father's name from suspicion. Already I've heard these ugly rumors whispered about everywhere. Nothing would set them at rest, unless I were to say that I myself had sent Blewitt away to his home in London."

"That would not be true."

"But it would save your father's reputation."

Freda said nothing. Her mistrust of this man made her shrewd. After a long pause she turned and looked straight into his face.

"Why do you tell *me* this?"

"I wanted to know whether you would care to have your father's name cleared."

"Not in such a way as that. I believe the best thing for my poor father would be for the whole truth to come out, and though the falsehood might seem to protect his name for the time, it would do less real good than quietly waiting."

"Then you wouldn't do me any little favour, out of gratitude if I tried to shield his name?"

"Little favour! Oh! and what is that?"

"For instance, you wouldn't get Crispin Bean to deal with us instead of with Josiah Kemm?"

"No!" flashed out the girl, "neither with you, nor Kemm, nor anybody else. The Abbey's mine now, and I won't have it used for *smuggling*, Mr. Heritage."

Robert started violently, and his hand shook as he played with his riding-whip.

"You are ready to accuse your own father of doing wrong then?"

"I don't make any accusations, Mr. Heritage. I only tell you that the Abbey is under my rule, now."

"You think so, perhaps; but you will find yourself mistaken. The trade will go on just the same whatever orders you may give; and it will make no difference if I have to go away, and if my cousin Dick, who brought you in out of the snow and was so good to you, has to starve."

Freda moved uneasily and shot a furtive glance at Dick, who was outside the old walls, apparently absorbed in unpleasant thoughts. Robert perceived the expression on the girl's face, its coy pity and maidenly fear. This vein, so happily struck, would bear a little further working, he thought.

"Yes," he went on. "Poor Dick! It has always been his lot to have a rough time of it. When he told me this morning of the impression you had made upon him, and asked me to put in a word for him with you if I got a chance, I knew it would be of no use. Not that he isn't a good-looking, good-hearted fellow enough, but because he is Dick, and never has any luck!"

The girl's face underwent many changes as she listened to this speech. Compassion, surprise, pleasure, confusion, annoyance—all flitted over her ingenious countenance, until at the end, suddenly perceiving that Robert's small light eyes were fixed upon her with great intentness, she blushed and turned away from him even haughtily.

"I do not believe that he asked you to speak to me!" she said.

"You don't? Well, I'll fetch him and make him speak for himself."

"No, no, no," cried the girl, crimson with confusion and distress. "I am going indoors. I—I am tired, cold. Good-morning, Mr. Heritage."

While Freda was crossing the meadow which lay between the ruin and the Abbey-house, she saw Nell at an upper window, watching her with an uneasy expression of face; by the time she reached the side-door, the housekeeper was there to admit her.

"Who was that I saw you talking to up there in the ruins?" asked Nell sharply. "Come, I know, for I saw you."

"Why do you ask me then?"

"After all the trouble I've taken too, to prevent those young rascals getting at you! Why, they've been pulling the bell nearly off every day and sometimes twice a day."

"Oh, they've been to see me before then?"

"Yes, at least Bob Heritage has, and everybody knows what a nice acquaintance *he* is for a young girl! But they won't see any more of you, if I can help it. A pretty mess I should get myself into if they did!"

Freda passed into the house and, without waiting for another word, went straight into the library, which was in the west wing, away from the rest of the inhabited part. The fire was burning very low, and the room looked cold, dusty and forlorn. A great pile of the books with which she had been amusing herself the night before still lay undisturbed on the hearth-rug. The books had almost become living friends to her, in the absence of sympathetic human beings. She threw herself down beside them and rested her arms on a stack of calf-bound histories and biographies.

What had Robert Heritage meant by those words about the "impression," she had made on Dick, and "putting in a good word for him." Innocent as she was, Freda could scarcely misunderstand the drift of these expressions, and they roused a thought which brought the blood to her cheeks, all alone as she was, and stirred her strangely. She did not believe Robert; who was she, a little lame girl, to rouse any deep interest in a big, strong, handsome man like Dick? And with a sigh, the girl sat up among her books and tried to stir the log fire into a blaze.

As she did so, a loud knocking on the wall behind her made her look round. The whole of the side of the room from which the sound came was filled with book-shelves from floor to ceiling. The knocking went on, until suddenly Freda saw some of the books begin to shake in a surprising manner, and a minute later six rows of books began to move slowly forward, and then a face peered out from behind them. It was that of Dick Heritage. Then she perceived that the books which he had appeared to disturb were sham ones, mere leather backs pasted on a door introduced among the genuine ones.

"How did you come in?" asked Freda in a husky whisper.

"By a way you don't know of," answered the young fellow, looking at his riding-whip.

"You came in to see me?" asked Freda in a softer tone.

"Yes," said Dick, suddenly standing erect, speaking in a full, firm voice, and looking straight up at the dusty ceiling with flashing blue eyes, "I came to see you, to speak to you about what that rascal Bob said. He told you something about me, didn't he? He made up some ridiculous nonsense that I'd said about you?"

Freda, with her little head bending lower and lower, nodded an affirmative very slowly.

"Well, there wasn't a word of truth in it. I never said anything of the sort. He only said it to serve his own interests. I was obliged to come and tell you the moment he confessed to me what he'd done. I didn't wish you to think me a fool or a knave."

Freda did not answer. When at last, after a long pause, Dick glanced at her, he perceived that she was quietly crying. Dick looked closer, in surprise and consternation.

"You're not crying, are you?" asked he uneasily.

Freda shook her head. Rising from her chair, she picked up an armful of the books that were scattered about the floor, and carrying them back to the shelves, began to replace them very deliberately. Dick, putting down his whip, followed with another load, which she took from him so hastily and awkwardly that they all dropped on the floor.

"I hope it's not anything in what I said, or the way I said it, that made you cry?"

He had gone down on one knee to pick up the fallen books, and he looked up into her face with an expression which seemed to Freda most touching.

"I am not crying, Mr. Heritage," she said, trying to be very dignified; "and I quite understand that you were not so foolish as to say that I had made a pleasant impression on you."

Dick dropped the books, and looked up at her with curiosity, compassion, and a little admiration. For although her eyes and nose were red with crying, she looked rather pretty as well as very pitiful.

"Oh," he said, laughing with some embarrassment, "it's not fair to put it like that now, is it?"

"That is all that your cousin said to me about you."

"No! Really? He told me that he said, implied rather, that I was making up to you, wanted you to marry me, in fact."

Freda blushed crimson.

"He never said anything like that to me," she said, "if he had, I should have known it was not true."

Dick sprang up eagerly.

"Yes, you would, wouldn't you? You would have known it was impossible such an idea should enter my head!"

Freda turned away and very quietly re-arranged some of the books she had placed on the shelves.

"Oh, yes;" and she laughed with some bitterness but more sadness. "Did you think it possible that I, who am lame, and fit for nothing but a convent, where I can pray, and can work with my needle as well as the strong ones, should ever put myself on an equality with the girls who can dance, and ride, and row?"

Dick was overwhelmed. In her innocence, as she had misunderstood his cousin, so she was misunderstanding him.

"Now look here, Miss Mulgrave," said he, as he brought his right hand heavily down on one of the bookshelves. "You are quite wrong. You have mistaken Bob's meaning and mine altogether. Don't you see that what he wanted was to get some sort of hold on you through me, since he couldn't get it in any other way? And can't you understand how mean it would be of me, and absurd (mean if I had any chance, and absurd as I haven't) to come to you and talk about admiration and love and marriage, when I am just in the position of a farm-labourer about to be turned off?"

"What do you mean?"

"Why, that your father's refusal to—to have anything more to do with us has ruined us; so that Bob and my aunt will have to leave the farm and go to London."

"And you, what will you do?"

"I shall stay on at the old place."

"But, you won't be comfortable!"

"More comfortable than I should be anywhere else. You see I'm not like the others, who just came to the old place when they had to let the Hall. I was brought up at the farm, and used to spend my holidays there. I was only annexed by my aunt and Bob when there was some dirty work to be done and it was seen that I might prove useful."

Dick's voice was so sweet and he spoke so very quietly that it was not until some minutes after he had finished this short autobiography that Freda perceived all the bitterness he had expressed in it.

"Oh!" she sighed out at last, in a voice full of soft reproach. "How could you?"

Dick laughed a little.

"I don't think I could make you understand. You are too good. I wish none of this business had ever come to your ears."

Freda looked thoughtful for a few minutes. Then she said:

"I don't wish that. You see I've been obliged to think a great deal lately, and I see that there is a great deal more wickedness and unhappiness in the world than we in the convent ever thought of. And it seems to me that to shut oneself up out of it all and to try to make a little heaven for oneself and to keep apart from all the difficulties and miseries outside is selfish. So that I'm glad I can't be so selfish any longer."

"Now I don't quite agree with you. By coming out you only add to the general sum of misery in the world by one more miserable unit; where's the advantage to your fellow-creatures of that?"

"But I don't intend to be miserable. I am going to try to bring some of the convent's happiness and peace to the people outside, or at least to—some of them."

"I should like to know how you propose to set about it."

"First, I am going to try to persuade—some people to give up doing what is wrong. I am going to try to persuade *you*."

"To give up——"

"Well, Free Trade."

"And make a virtue of necessity? You see, *it* has given *me* up."

"Did you like—doing that?"

"Smuggling? You called it smuggling this morning, and now that it has nothing more to do with me, I don't mind if I give it the same name. I was first mixed up with it when I was seventeen, before the age when one grows either a beard or a conscience, and I can't honestly say that I felt anything but enjoyment of the excitement."

"Your cousin led you into it?"

"Well, I suppose so. Somebody else led him."

Her face fell.

"I know—my father."

"And it went on for a long time, and one got used to the risk and took that as a set-off against the wrong. And after all, we were only carrying out with logical thoroughness the blessed theory of Free Trade, of which we are told we ought as a nation to be so proud. It has ruined us small land-owners, by making it impossible to cultivate the land remuneratively. Who can blame us then if we try to get compensation by taking a hair out of the tail of the dog that bit us?"

"I can't argue with you, because I don't know enough. But I suppose the laws are on the whole good and just, and it is right to obey them. It must be bad for people to live always under the feeling that they have to hide something."

"Why, what bad effect has it had upon me? Have you found me such a very redoubtable ruffian?"

"Oh, no! Oh, no; you have been very good and kind."

"Well, certainly I have wished nothing but good to you. I came with Bob this morning only to see that he didn't bully you, and if in any way I could help you or get you away out of this place, I would. Is that rough brute Crispin kind to you?"

"Yes, and no. He is very strange. Sometimes he is harsh and hard and so disagreeable I scarcely dare speak to him, and then at other times he will be almost tender."

"He hasn't got tipsy yet, and frightened you?"

"Tipsy! Oh, no!" cried Freda half in alarm and half in indignation. "I don't believe he would. I am sure he wouldn't," she added warmly.

"You speak as if you were quite fond of him," said Dick, surprised and laughing.

"So I am, rather. Somehow I can't help thinking he is fond of me. It is very strange."

"I don't think so. I don't think it strange that any one seeing a good deal of you should get fond of you. Well," he added after a pause, during which they both reddened and looked rather embarrassed, "and have you tried yet to convert Crispin to your views upon smuggling?"

"Crispin! Oh, no, I should be afraid."

"I see, you respect him more than you do me. You think he may smuggle from conscientious conviction? For I may tell you that he is the right hand in all these enterprises, so that they can go on as well without the Captain as with him, if only Crispin is there."

"I know that."

She paused a moment and then went on: "I haven't seen him the last few days. When I do I have something to say to him which will stop his smuggling too, I think."

"Why, what's that!"

Freda raised her finger in sign of caution, not without a little air of importance.

"There is a man about here sent by government to look after the smuggling: I'm going to tell him that."

Dick's face changed, and became full of excitement and interest.

"Why, how came you to hear of such a thing? Are you sure of it?"

"Quite sure. I have seen him, talked with him. He is a great friend of mine."

"Then if he is, I warn you most solemnly to tell him not to interfere with these men, nor to let them know what he's up to. They're an awfully rough lot, these fellows. Only the Captain, and Crispin Bean, who's been captain of the yacht so long, can manage them."

"The yacht!" cried Freda. "Why, that is used for the smuggling then!"

"Oh, I don't know that," answered Dick hastily. "But, but—if you don't want to hear of any more mysterious deaths and disappearances in the neighbourhood, remember to warn your friend. Now I must go; good-bye."

He held out his hand abruptly, but withdrew it with a shy laugh before Freda could take it.

"Perhaps you would rather not shake hands with such a rascal."

"Oh," said Freda naïvely, as she held out both hers, "that doesn't matter. For all the men I know seem to be rascals."

Dick laughed, but did not seem to like this observation. He drew himself up a little, and a variety of emotions seemed to chase each other across his face.

"I'm glad my poor mother isn't alive to hear me called *that*," he said in a low voice.

Freda ran up to him, but stopped herself shyly as she was going to take his hand.

"You used the word first, and I didn't mean it seriously," she whispered, in great distress. "You could not think me so ungrateful."

"Oh, I didn't mean to put on airs and pretend to be insulted. But perhaps I am not so bad as you think. At any rate, if I do wrong, there's a comfort in knowing I get punished for it."

CHAPTER XVIII.

DICK disappeared through the door by which he had entered so quickly that before Freda had had time to utter more than an exclamation, the rows of real books and sham ones were again unbroken, and the noise of a drawn bolt told her that it was of no use for her to try to follow him.

She sat down again in a tumult of agitated feelings. Her heart felt drawn out to this young fellow with what she thought must be gratitude for his kindness. She looked with vivid interest at the various spots in the room on which he had stood, and tried to imagine his figure in them again. She even crossed to the bookshelves, and laid her hand on the place where his had lain, and touched again the books which he had handed to her. She felt so sorry for him, so sure that in his share of the wicked enterprise of his cousin and her father, Dick had been little more than a victim. And then these musings gave place to more serious thoughts. She had two duties to perform; one was to tell Crispin that there really was a government emissary on the look out, the other was to warn John Thurley not to betray himself. This latter duty was, however, clearly impossible for her to fulfil without the aid of accident; but the former might be easier.

Now during all this time that Crispin had kept himself invisible to her eyes, the night-noises which had alarmed Freda so much at first had been continued regularly, with only this difference: that although she had crept out to watch the panel-door in the gallery, no one had passed through it, and no one had been visible in the courtyard. It seemed clear then, to the girl, that there must be, as Dick had said, some entrance to the house which she did not know of. To ascertain this beyond a doubt, she laid an ingenious plan, and night having by this time fallen, she proceeded to carry it out. For if, she said to herself, she could once find the door by which the nocturnal exits and entrances were made, she would not only be able to waylay Crispin as he came in or went out, but would have a very important weapon in her hand by this knowledge.

Freda had seen, in a corner of Mrs. Bean's wash-house, a heap of silver sand. Watching her opportunity, she filled her skirt with this, slipped out, and making a careful tour of the house, stables, and outbuildings, she put two narrow lines of the sand before every door, including that by which Crispin had once carried her into the house. The snow had by this time melted or been swept away from the neighbourhood of all buildings, and in such places the ground had dried sufficiently for her purpose. To do her work the more thoroughly, she then went the round of the outer walls of the garden and enclosures, and repeated her sand-strewing before every door she found, and before the iron entrance gates. Then she crept back into the house, feeling pretty sure that she had been unseen in the moonless night, and went to bed, tired but full of excitement.

She was too restless to sleep, so presently she got up again, put on her dressing-gown, and waited eagerly for a repetition of the usual sounds. She was soon satisfied: first the distant mutterings, far underneath her feet, then the mounting of slow feet up stone steps; the voices subdued, but nearer; the moving of heavy burdens; a sound of weights falling; the chink of glasses; a low murmur of talk in men's voices, the sounds gradually dying away. That was all. An hour, by the little clock on her mantelpiece, from the first sound to the last. Then all was quiet till morning, when Freda, after a disturbed night of short snatches of sleep, woke with a start to the memory of her undertaking. Ah! She had got them now! In an hour she would know all about it; she would be able to waylay and confront them, if she chose. And she almost thought she would choose.

Full of these ideas, Freda dressed hastily and ran downstairs. Nell was busy in the kitchen; the place was as deserted as usual. She stole out of the house with a loudly beating heart, feeling refreshed instead of chilled by the air of the keen March morning. Stealthily, with one eye on Nell's quarters and one on her task, she began her tour, her excitement increasing as door after door was reached, and there was still no sign.

At last the tour was made, the inspection ended, in bitter disappointment.

For the sand before every door was undisturbed.

CHAPTER XIX.

THE discovery of the fact that there was a secret way in and out of the Abbey had a strong and most unhappy effect upon poor Freda. She dared not say anything about it to Nell, and Crispin she never saw: forced, therefore, to bear the burden of the secret alone, she crept about the house day by day, not daring to make any fresh researches, and suffering from a hundred fears. To add to her unhappiness, she now could not but feel sure that Nell had kept back her letter to Sister Agnes. For she got no answer to it. Mrs. Bean seemed to guess that the girl had learned something about which she would want to ask inconvenient questions. So Freda passed a week in silence and solitude such as the convent had not accustomed her to. Even the nocturnal noises had ceased. Once, and once only, she caught sight of Crispin, and ran after him, calling him by name. It was dusk, and she was watching the sea-mews from the courtyard, as they flew screaming about the desolate walls of what had once been the banqueting-room. He did not answer, but disappeared rapidly under the gallery in evident avoidance of her.

Poor Freda felt so desolate that she burst into tears. Her old, fanciful belief in her father was dead. Everything pointed to the fact that he was really Blewitt's murderer, and that, in order to save himself from detection, he had feigned death and gone away without one thought of the daughter he was deserting. Now that Crispin, whom she had looked upon through all as her friend, was deserting her also, she grew desperate, and recovering all the courage which for the last few days had seemed dead in her, she resolved to make another attempt to fathom the secrets the Abbey still held from her.

To begin with, she must explore the west wing. Now this west wing was so dark and so cold, so honeycombed with narrow little passages which seemed to lead to nowhere in particular, and with small rooms meagrely furnished and full of dust, that Freda had always been rather afraid of lingering about it, and had hopped through so much of it as she was obliged to pass on her way to and from the library, with as much speed as possible. Now, however, she got a candle, and boldly proceeded to examine every nook and corner of the west wing. And the result of her researches was to prove that on the ground floor, underneath her own room, there was a chamber surrounded by four solid stone walls without a single doorway or window. The only entrance to this mysterious chamber seemed to be through the panel-door in the storey above. Where, then, did the secret door in the library lead to? That question she would solve at once. It was quite dark and very cold in the narrow passages through which she ran, and the tipity-tap of her crutch frightened her by the echo it awoke. She reached the library panting, and running to the secret door, began pulling it and shaking it with all her might.

Suddenly the door gave way, almost throwing her down as it opened upon her; with a cry she recognised Dick behind it. She had thought of him so much since his last strange appearance, that the sight of him in the flesh made her feel shy. She said nothing, but crept away towards the window, feeling indeed an overwhelming joy at the sight of a friendly face.

"Did I frighten you again?" asked he.

The girl turned and looked up at him, shyly.

"I am always frightened here," she said.

"Poor child! They are treating you very badly. I was afraid so. I have been to see you twice, to make sure you had come to no harm."

Freda, who had crept into the window-seat, as far away from him as she could get, looked up in surprise.

"You have been to see me?" she exclaimed.

"Not to see you exactly, because the door was shut between us. But I heard you in here, talking to yourself and turning over the leaves of your books. I didn't think it worth while to disturb you. I shouldn't have come in to-night, only I heard you shaking and pulling the door, and I thought you had heard me and were frightened."

"Oh, no. I wanted to know where it led to."

"To the floor above by a staircase. See."

He opened the door through which he had entered, and showed her the lowest steps of a very narrow staircase, which went up along the outer side of the library-wall.

"And how did you get into the floor above?"

"Well, it's a secret I'm bound not to betray."

"It doesn't matter," said Freda coolly, "I shall find it out. I want them to find that I am a meddlesome, inquisitive creature, who must be got rid of."

"Who's 'them'?" asked Dick.

"Crispin and Mrs. Bean."

"And you want them to send you back to the convent?"

"Yes."

"I think that would be a pity."

"You didn't last time."

"No-o," said Dick, clearing his throat. "Perhaps I didn't see it quite so well then. You see I hadn't thought about it. But I have since; and there's a lot in what you said about the selfishness of it."

"Ah, but now I'm just in the only position in the world in which it isn't selfish. I am quite alone, you see."

"So you were a week ago."

"But I had some hope then that I might be able to do some good. Now I haven't. And you don't know what it is to be always lonely, to have nobody to speak to even. It makes one feel like an outcast from all the world."

"Yes, so it does. So that one is glad of the very mice that run behind the wainscot; and when one of the little brutes comes out of its hole and runs about the room, why one wouldn't disturb it for the world."

"Oh, yes, I love the mice. Do you know I expect that sometimes when I have listened to a scratching in the wall and thought it was mice, it was really you all the time!"

"Very likely."

"It was very good of you to come and see that I was all right."

"Oh, I was glad to come. I'm lonely too now. They've gone away, the others."

"Your aunt, and your cousin? And left you all by yourself?"

"*That* wouldn't be much of a hardship, if only one could manage to exist. But it is lonely, as you say. I shouldn't mind it if the dog wouldn't howl so. Sign of a death, they say; I shouldn't be sorry if it were mine."

"Your death! Oh, don't say that. You didn't seem at all miserable when I went to your house."

"No. The fact is, *you* are at the bottom of my low spirits. It's your uncanny spells that have done it, Miss Mulgrave. Witches always have little sticks like that."

He took up her crutch almost reverently. It was leaning against the window-seat between them, for he had sat down beside her.

"What do you mean, Dick?"

It was only a consequence of her extreme ignorance of the world's ways that she called him by the name by which she had heard others call him. But it came upon the young man as a startling and delicious surprise.

"Why, I mean," he said, with rather more apparent constraint than before, "that you said things which made me uncomfortable, preached me a little sermon, in fact."

"Oh, I beg your pardon; I did not mean to preach indeed."

"It's all right, it did me good. I don't mind a girl preaching, and I thought over what you said very seriously. I—" he hesitated, and then finished hurriedly, "I thought you'd like to know."

"Indeed I'm very glad, if you didn't think me rude. Perhaps if my preaching did you good, it might do Crispin good too—if only I could get hold of him."

Dick laughed.

"I don't think I should set my heart too much upon that. Crispin is a thorough-paced old rascal."

"You don't know him. You haven't seen into his heart," cried Freda, rising from the window-seat in her earnestness, and bending forward so that she might look into the young man's face. For very little light now came through the old mullioned window.

"Well, I don't believe he has a heart to see into."

"Ah, that is because you have been careless, and have neglected your religion. We all, even the worst, have a heart; it may sleep sometimes, so that men think it is dead. But if God sends some one, with love for Him alive and glowing, to speak to that sleeping heart, it awakens, and a little spark of love and goodness will shine bright in it. Don't you believe that?"

"I believe that if anybody could work miracles through goodness, it would be you. But it would take a thundering big miracle to make Crispin Bean anything but an unprincipled rascal. Why, if you only knew—— But then it's better you should not know," said he, pulling himself up hurriedly and getting up to go.

"Oh, tell me, do tell me. I want to know!"

"You wouldn't be a woman if you didn't. But I'm not going to tell you."

And Dick drew himself up and looked out of the window, with the obstinate look she had seen before on his face. Freda was far too unconscious of her own feminine powers to attempt to move his resolution. She only sighed as he held out his hand.

"Are you very lonely at the farm?" she asked.

"Very. At least I mean *rather*."

"You have nobody there at all to speak to?"

"Nobody at all."

"And you will go on living like that?"

"As long as I can hold out. The love of the old place, and of all this country round, is a passion with me—the only one I've ever had, in fact. And you," he continued, leaving the subject of his own prospects with some abruptness, "you are lonely too. May I come and see you again?"

Freda hesitated.

"May I not come? Don't you want to see me again?"

"Oh, yes. But——"

"I don't frighten you, do I, with my rough, uncivilised ways?"

"Oh, no; Oh, no. Frighten me! Of course not."

"Then, if I don't frighten you, why did you screw yourself up into a corner of the window-seat just now, to be as far from me as possible?"

He spoke in a low tone, bending towards her.

Freda blushed, but she never thought of denying the accusation. But what had her reason been? She herself did not know.

"I—I think it must have been because I had been crying, and of course nobody likes to be seen crying," she answered slowly, hoping that she had told the truth.

"Crying, had you? What about? Tell me just this: is it about—Blewitt's—death?"

"Why, why, do you know anything about that?"

"I know," said Dick cautiously, "that it had something to do with your father's—disappearance."

Freda shivered at the word.

"You know more than that?" she said hoarsely.

"Perhaps. But I swear I can't tell *you* what I know, so don't ask me."

For a minute there was dead silence, as they stood face to face, but scarcely able to see each other in the gathering darkness. Suddenly both were startled by the sound of a man's hoarse voice, muffled by distance, which seemed to come from behind the door, through which Dick had entered.

CHAPTER XX.

AT first both Dick and Freda listened to the faint sounds in silence. Then Dick spoke.

"They've come back. I sha'n't be able to get out that way," he said.

"Why should you? I can let you out by the front-gate."

"But—I don't want to be seen," he said. "If Captain Mulgrave were to see me——"

Freda was startled by this suggestion, which betrayed how much the young man knew or guessed. She turned from the door, where she had paused with her fingers on the handle.

"Oh, yes," he said in a low voice and very quickly, understanding her thought, "it did take me in, for a time, and my cousin Bob too, that story about his being dead, although we both knew him very well."

"But why should he pretend any such thing?"

"That's what we want to find out. It makes us careful. So Bob's gone away, and I keep watch."

"And you are so sure he is alive?"

"I've seen him."

Freda began to tremble. Here was an answer to the question she had so often asked herself, whether her father was not really in hiding about the place after all. She led the way out of the library, along the corridor and out into the courtyard by the nearest door, without a word. It was so dark that there was little fear of their being seen crossing to the gate; though indeed Freda had forgotten that there was need of caution, being absorbed in conjectures about her father. She took the big key from its nail, opened the heavy gate, and led Dick through to the open space before the blank wall of the banqueting-hall. They crossed this, still in silence, and came to the lodge. Here she was about to summon the lodge-keeper, when Dick stopped her.

"Don't," said he. "The old woman would recognise me, and you would be made to suffer. I must get out some other way."

"There is no other way," said Freda. "And when my friends come to see me they should go out by the front way."

And, before he could stop her, she had seized the iron bell-handle which hung outside the wall of the lodge and rang it firmly.

The old woman who kept the key looked rather frightened when she saw who was with Freda, but she unlocked the gate, waited, curtseying, while the young people shook hands, and then popped back into her cottage like a rabbit.

But there were eyes about more to be dreaded than the old woman's. When Freda returned to the inner gate, which she had left open, she found it locked, and had to ring the bell. Mrs. Bean did not answer the summons for some time, and when she did, it was with a frown of ill-omen upon her face.

"So you've been receiving visitors, I see," she began shortly.

"Yes, I've had one visitor."

"One of the young Heritages, whom your father specially wished you not to have anything to do with. Crispin told you that."

"Yes," said Freda tremulously, "but since they leave me here all by myself with nobody to speak to, they can't be surprised if I make any friends when I can."

"Well, and am I not friend enough for you, without your having to run after any stranger or vagabond that happens to come into the parish?"

"No, you're not, for I certainly couldn't say anything I liked to you, as one can to a friend. If I ask you a question, you put me off with an answer that tells me nothing, as if I were a child. But I'm going to show you that I'm grown up, and do some things that will astonish you."

And Freda hopped quickly away across the court-yard to the entrance of the west wing, leaving Nell a little anxious and perturbed by this new independence.

Freda returned to the study, her little brain actively spinning fancies concerning her late visitor, all of a pretty, harmless kind, dowering him with a great many ideal qualities to which the young man could certainly not lay claim. It was now so dark in the room that she had to feel her way carefully, well as she knew it. She walked along close by the wall, touching the book-laden shelves as she went, until she came to a point where they seemed to yield under her fingers. Her heart leapt up. This was the secret door through which Dick had entered: and he had left it open.

Freda's first impulse was delight; her second fear. Now that the way was at last open to her to learn the secrets of this guilty house, she began to shrink from the knowledge she was about to gain. She opened the door, listened, and looked in. Pitch-black darkness; utter silence. She knew that Dick had come down by a staircase, so she felt for it and mounted carefully. She counted fourteen rather steep steps, and then she found that she had reached a level floor. It was so cold here that her hands and feet were stiff and benumbed, although her head was burning; she was in a passage the walls of which were of stone, just like those outside her own room. But this passage was narrower, she thought. There was no light whatever, so that she groped her way cautiously, with her left hand outstretched before her face, while with the right she tapped her crutch lightly on the ground in front of her. After a few steps she came to a blank stone wall; it was the end of the passage and she had to turn back. As she retraced her steps, she suddenly came to a slight recess on the right hand, where the stone wall was broken by a wooden door. Something in the sound of this as she rattled it made her believe that this was the panel-door into the gallery. If this were so, the way down was through a trap-door in the floor; for this was the way Crispin had brought her on the day that he found her in the disused stable. Down she went upon her knees, feeling about until her hand touched an end of knotted rope. Pulling this up, she found, as she had expected, that it raised a door in the floor, beneath which was a flight of wooden steps. There was still no sound to be heard, so, after a moment's hesitation, she decided to continue her explorations, and to trust to luck to hide herself if she heard any one coming. The steps were rickety, but she got down them in safety, and found herself in a stone passage, similar to that on the floor above. At the end of this was a door, which Freda, still groping in the dark, decided to be that which opened into one of the out-houses in the yard outside. It was securely fastened. She felt her way back along the walls until a door on the right suddenly gave way under her hand, and a flash of light, after the darkness in which she had been so long, streamed into her eyes and dazzled her.

Freda thought she was discovered; but the utter silence reassuring her, she presently looked up again, and found that she was standing before the doorway of a big, stone-walled, windowless room, piled high with bales and boxes which reeked with the unmistakable odour of strong tobacco. She was in the smugglers' storeroom. An oil-lamp, which hung opposite to the door and gave a bright light, enabled her to make an exhaustive survey of the room and its contents. In one corner there was a rope and pulley fastened securely to one of the strong beams which ran from end to end of the roof. There was no ceiling. Directly under this rope and pulley was a square hole in the floor; and Freda, peeping down, saw that a rope-ladder connected this chamber with another underneath, which, however, was unlighted. She had scarcely had time to make these discoveries when she heard dull, muffled sounds which seemed to come from beneath the cellar. Afraid of being caught by one of the unknown men whose coarse voices she had so often heard, Freda hid herself among the bales not far from the opening in the floor. The sounds came nearer, became distinguishable as the tramp of one man's feet, and then the rope-ladder began to shake.

Freda, peeping out, began to tremble at her own daring. The man was coming up, and already she knew, whether by instinct or by his tread she hardly could tell, that it was not Crispin. She shrank back, with a loudly-beating heart, and crouched behind the bales as the newcomer reached the floor and pulled up the rope-ladder after him. He began to move some of the bales, and Freda was half dead with fear lest he should touch those behind which she was hiding. But presently he desisted from this work, and she heard him drag out a heavy weight from the space he had made, draw a cork, and presently began to take long breaths of pleasure and to smack his lips. Very cautiously, believing him to be too agreeably employed to notice her, she then dared to peep at him. But the sight of his face turned her sick with surprise and dread.

For she saw the grinning, withered face she had seen about the house in the darkness, the face which Nell had tried to persuade her was the creation of her imagination.

CHAPTER XXI.

FREDA fancied that the long-drawn breath which escaped her as she recognised the man must attract his attention. But he was too intent upon the enjoyment of the strong spirit, which he kept pouring from a huge stone bottle into a cracked tumbler, to have eyes or ears for the little eavesdropper in the corner. A horrible idea flashed into her mind as she crouched again in her hiding-place: Was this grinning creature, with the hideous face of an ape, the father she had waited to know so long? A shiver of horror ran through her as she remembered how this would tally with the facts she knew: with the dread in which her father was held, with her belief that he was in hiding about the house, and with the airs of proprietorship which this man was assuming.

Even as these unwelcome thoughts pressed into her mind, the man got up, and confirming her fears by his tone of authority, stamped upon the floor and called down the opening in a loud voice:

"Hallo! Anybody there yet? Kelk! Harrison!"

There was no answer, and he walked up and down, swearing to himself impatiently. Presently a muffled sound came from below, and he called out again.

"Aye, aye, sir," said a hoarse voice.

"Is that you, Braim?" asked the man above.

"Aye, sir."

"Anybody else with you?"

"Theer be fower on us, sir."

"All right. Close up, and I'll be down with you in a minute."

There were sounds now in the cellar below of several men moving about and talking in low tones. Then the man above moved back a step or two from the opening in the floor; and Freda, whose curiosity had grown stronger than her caution, peeped out far enough to see him take from a shelf a small revolver, which he secreted about his person. Then he lowered the rope-ladder, let himself down into the cellar by it, and immediately threw it up again so deftly that it landed safely on the floor he had left. Freda heard a chorus of demands for "soomat to warm them," and by the sounds which followed she could soon tell that drinking had begun. Being now able to lift her head without fear, she could make out a good deal of their talk, although the strong dialect in which all but the leader spoke often puzzled her. As the talk went on and the drink went round, the men seemed to get more and more excited; but just as they had done at the "Barley Mow," they lowered their voices as they grew warm in discussion, until Freda, whose interest and curiosity had become deeply excited, crept softly out of her hiding-place, and crawling to the opening in the floor, listened with her head only just out of the men's sight.

They were talking about some person against whom they had a grudge, using oaths and threats which, although strange and new to Freda, shocked her by their coarseness. At last her curiosity to see them grew so great that she was impelled to glance down stealthily at the group below. The men were seated at a rough deal table, over which they leaned and sprawled, with their heads close together, in eager converse. It was some moments before she got a view of any of the faces; at last, however, two of them raised their heads a little, and she instantly recognised one as a little wrinkled, oldish-looking man, who wore rings in his ears and walked with the cat-like tread of one accustomed to go barefoot, whom she had seen at the "Barley Mow."

"Ah tell ye," he was now saying, "it's' t' same now as were at t' 'Barley Mow' on t' neght when train was snawed oop. Barnaby Ugthorpe fund him aht, and tawd me abaht it hissen."

Freda forgot to draw back; her breath came with difficulty: this man against whom they were using such hideous threats must be her friend, John Thurley. From this moment, every word they uttered assumed for her a terrible significance.

"Oh, I've no doubt your information is right enough," said the leader, who used fewer words than the rest, "the question is whether he hasn't found out too much for it to be any good interfering with him. You see, he's been about the neighbourhood some time now, keeping very quiet, and he may have picked up and sent off to London enough information to do for all the lot of us; in that case a bullet or two through his hide would only increase the unpleasantness of our position."

"Aye, aye, Captain, but Ah've kep' a eye upon him, to see what he were up to. A pal of mine done that business for me, an' as fur as we mak' aht, he hasn't done mooch correspondering, an' nothing suspicious-loike. Ah've a pal in t' poast-office, as Ah have moast pleaces, an' ye can tak' my word for't."

"An' now we've fahnd him aht spying at us from t' scaur, as we did yesterneght, Ah seay it's high toime as a stop wur put to his goings on, an' it's not loike ye, Capt'n, to seay neay to that."

"I don't say nay to that," said the little withered man, with an ugly grin on his face. "You know me better. But no good ever comes of using violent means until you've tried all others. I'll be on the scaur myself to-night and watch."

Freda stared down at the group, fascinated with horror. There was a brutal callousness of look and tone in these men which made her feel as if she were watching a cageful of wild beasts. Every line of their weather-beaten faces, dimly as she saw them by the light of two flaring tallow candles, seemed to her to be eloquent of the risks and dangers of a hardening and brutalising life. And the face which looked the most repulsive of all was that of the leader. Was he her father? The girl prayed that it might not be true. Although his speech was so much more correct than that of the rest as to mark him as belonging to a higher class, his voice was coarse and thick, and his manner furtive and restless. Even the faint twinkle of humour which was visible in the eyes of the wizened informer, James Braim, was absent from those of his chief. Those few words, in which he said that he would watch on the scaur that night, filled Freda with more anxiety for John Thurley's safety than all the coarse threats and menacing gestures of the other three men.

"Goin' to unload to-night, Capt'n?" asked one man.

The leader nodded.

"Must. Here's three nights we've wasted hanging about, on account of the scare about this spy, whoever he is. So to-night you'll get to work, and I'll keep the lookout, and if anybody's fool enough to be loafing about where he's not wanted when he ought to be in bed, why, he can't in fairness complain if he gets—sent home."

He paused significantly before the last two words, and a low murmur of appreciation and amusement went round the group. Then the talk was carried on in short whispers, and Freda was presently seized with the fancy that some of the questions and answers exchanged referred to her. For the men talked about some woman, and all the questions were directed to the repulsive-looking leader, who after some minutes rose, with a remark a little louder than the previous talk.

"She won't interfere with any of us much longer, at any rate. We can't afford to keep spies in the camp. Now, lads, it's time for business. Get off to the yacht, and to business as fast as you can. I'll be down on the scaur in less than half an hour."

The men pushed back their seats without delay, Kelk alone venturing on a grumbling word of remonstrance. And then, still watching closely from above, Freda saw a very strange occurrence. The bare, ill-lighted cellar grew empty of all except the leader as if by magic, the men seeming to disappear into the bowels of the earth. As she looked, bending her head lower and lower with straining eyes to spy out the reason of this, Freda involuntarily drew a long breath of amazement. The solitary man left in the cellar looked up, as he was in the act of filling his own glass once more from the stone jar. The girl drew back with a cry, for a look of intense malignity passed over the man's wrinkled face.

"Hallo!" he exclaimed very quietly, blinking up at her, "so it's you, is it? Playing the spy as usual?"

He muttered an oath below his breath, and came close under the opening in the floor.

"Just throw down that rope," he continued peremptorily.

"What rope?" asked Freda, trembling.

"Come, you know well enough. You haven't got eyes in your head for nothing." He paused, but Freda remained motionless. "Now then," he added with a sudden access of anger and a stamp of his foot on the stone floor, "throw down the rope-ladder I came down by. Do you understand that?"

But Freda only attempted to get away. Excited by anger and drink, the man took from his belt a revolver, which he pointed up at her. This action, strangely enough, checked Freda's impulse to retreat. She looked down at him straightforwardly and fearlessly, eye to eye.

"Do you think you can make me obey you by shooting me?" she asked simply.

"I think you are a d——d ungrateful little chit," answered the man sullenly. But he lowered the weapon in his hand.

"Ungrateful!" faltered Freda, the great fear rising again in her heart. "Ungrateful!" she repeated. "Then you are—are you—my father?"

"Of course I am," he answered sullenly. "Pretty filial instincts you seem to have!"

Freda was overwhelmed. For a few moments she sat transfixed, looking down on this newly-found parent with undisguised horror.

"Well, aren't you going to obey me?" repeated he with rather less ferocity of tone.

"Yes," whispered Freda hoarsely.

She drew back a step or two from the opening in the floor, and began to grope about with cold, clammy fingers for the rope-ladder. At last she found it and threw it down.

If she had not been so benumbed with amazement and grief at this discovery, she would have been frightened by the savage exclamation with which the man set his foot on the ladder. As it was, she heard nothing, saw nothing until she suddenly felt herself pulled up by the arm. Dragged to her feet against her will, paralysed with alarm, she turned to see the grinning, withered face held close to hers, full of spite and malignity.

"Now," said he, "I'm going to give you a lesson for your disobedience."

With a shudder and a low cry, Freda struggled with him, avoiding the meeting with his eyes.

"Don't," she whispered hoarsely. "Don't. I wish to remember my obedience, my duty. I can't if you treat me like a dog."

He gave a short, rasping laugh.

"I sha'n't do that," he said. "I respect a dog."

At the brutal words and tone, Freda, by a sudden movement, wrenched herself free for an instant, and looked him steadily in the face.

"Now," she said, "I know that you have been deceiving me. You are not my father!"

"We'll see about that. Come here."

He seized her by the right wrist, giving it such a violent twist that she cried out with pain. "Now if you struggle any more or cry out, I'll just give you a broken arm to match your broken leg."

He gave her arm another wrench to prove that his threat was not an idle one, and the girl with difficulty suppressed a moan. Just as he gripped her arm more tightly to inflict further punishment for this insubordination, a change came quite suddenly over his face; he dropped her arm at once, and sliding over the floor as stealthily and rapidly as a cat, he ran down the rope-ladder, and disappeared from view just as his four subordinates had done.

Freda was bewildered, and not one whit relieved at his disappearance. It only seemed to augur some fresh misfortune. As she stood where he had left her, dazed, miserable, still nursing her arm for the pain, she heard another step behind her. Her endurance had been tried too much; she could not face a fresh enemy, as she believed the newcomer to be. Putting her hands before her face, she turned and stepped backwards, away from him, murmuring broken entreaties, interrupted by sobs. As she retreated, she felt that the intruder was pursuing her, and fled faster and faster.

"Stop, child, stop," cried at last a voice she knew. At the same moment she felt that she had gone a step too far, and was falling through the opening in the floor. But even as she felt this, strong arms were thrown round her, and she found herself in a warm clasp of kindliness. Opening her eyes, she saw who her preserver was, saw too that his eyes were full of tenderness.

"Crispin! Crispin!" she cried.

But the next moment, with a wild shriek, she flung her arms round his neck in a passionate embrace.

"No, no, not Crispin, you are not really Crispin! You—are—*my father!*" she sobbed out with a burst of hysterical tears and laughter.

CHAPTER XXII.

NOT even the stolid silence with which he received her demonstrative outburst could dissuade Freda from her new belief that this man, whom she had always known as Crispin Bean, was really her father. She wondered, as she looked into his stern, rugged face, and noted the half involuntary tenderness in his eyes as he looked at her, how she could ever have doubted it. She chose to believe now that she had really known it all the time, and that she had only been waiting for him to declare himself. This, however, he was not ready to do even now.

"I am Crispin, Crispin," he said, while he patted her soothingly on the shoulder, "remember that."

He did not speak harshly, but even if he had done so she would not have been afraid of him. She was so overjoyed to have found her father, as she still obstinately believed she had done, that she was ready to submit to any condition it might be his fancy to impose.

"Yes, Crispin," she said meekly, nestling up to his shoulder and looking with shy gladness up in his face, "I will remember anything you tell me, Crispin."

He put his arm round her with a sudden impulse of tenderness, and Freda fancied, as he looked into her eyes, that he was trying to trace a resemblance to her mother; she fancied, too, by a look of content mingled with sadness which came over his face, that he succeeded.

"I heard you crying out as I came in," he said at last, abruptly. "Was it my footsteps that frightened you?"

"No," said Freda hesitatingly.

"What was it, then?"

"A man, a man I have seen about the house before, came up from there,"—she pointed to the hole in the floor—"and frightened me. *He* said he was my father."

Crispin looked black.

"How did he frighten you?" he asked shortly.

"He saw me looking through at him and some other men—dreadful looking men—who were talking together; and I think he was angry because I saw them. So he made me throw the rope down to him, and he came up, and he was very angry."

And Freda shuddered at the recollection.

"He didn't hurt you, threaten you, did he?"

She hesitated.

"Not much. Perhaps he didn't mean to hurt me at all, only to frighten me. But I *was* frightened."

And she hid her face against Crispin's shoulder.

"Jealous brute, he shall suffer for this!" he muttered angrily. Turning to her suddenly again he asked: "Did you hear what the other men said? Did they frighten you?"

"I didn't hear much, and none of them saw me except that one man. But, oh, Crispin, they are dreadful people! Why do you have anything to do with them?"

"Little girls shouldn't ask questions," he answered rather grimly.

But Freda would not take his tone as a warning. Indeed she had an object of vital importance at her heart.

"But there was something they said, something I did hear, which I must tell you about, even if I make you angry—Crispin. There is a man whom they want to hurt, perhaps to kill; they said so. They are going to be out on the scaur to-night, and if he is there, as they expect, the wicked man, the worst of them all, said he would be on the watch."

"Well, a man may watch another without hurting him. Like a foolish girl, who listens to what doesn't concern her, you have half-heard things, and jumped to a ridiculous conclusion."

But Freda was not to be put off like that. She rose from the bench on which they had been sitting side by side, and stood before him so that she could look straight into his face.

"No, no," she cried vehemently. "I know more than you think, and I know they meant harm to John Thurley, who was kind to me, and wanted me to go away because he thought I was lonely and not taken care of."

Crispin glanced up hastily, with a guilty flush on his face.

"Mrs. Bean—Nell looks after you, doesn't she?" he asked sharply.

"Oh," said the girl with a little half-bitter laugh, "I am fed all right; but perhaps Mr. Thurley thinks that food isn't quite all a girl wants."

Crispin got up abruptly, almost pushing her aside, and began walking about the room, as if in search of something to do, to hide a certain uneasiness which he felt. He kicked a coil of rope into a corner, and shifted one of the bales that had got a little out of place.

"I know," he burst out suddenly, "that I—that you have not been treated well. You have been neglected, shamefully neglected. Of course you ought never to have come. It was a mistake, a caprice of temper on the part of—your father. Then when you came, of course you ought to have been sent back; it was cruel and wrong to keep you here. But by that time—you had brought—something, a ray of humanity, perhaps, or of sunshine, to—somebody, and so you stayed. And—and of course it was wrong, and somebody—is sorry."

Freda, touched, breathless, was drinking in every word, with her great brown eyes fixed upon him. She flew up at the last words, and forgetting even her crutch, limped across to him and fell into his arms.

"Oh," she whispered, "but you should have said so, you should have told me! And then if you had wished me to live on here like this for a year, ten years, without ever even seeing your face, I would have done it gladly, if I had only known you cared, that it gave you one spark of comfort or satisfaction. Oh, you believe me, do you not?"

He could not help believing her, for truth and devotion were burning clear in her eyes. But it puzzled, it almost alarmed him.

"You—you are strangely, ridiculously sentimental," he said, trying to laugh. "How did you come by all these high-flown notions?"

"Whatever I feel God put into my heart, when he sent me to you to make you happy again, as you were when my mother was alive."

He half-pushed her away, with a sharply-drawn breath of pain; for she had touched the still sensitive place.

"Ah, child," he said, "they have educated you on fairy tales. There is no going back to peace and happiness and innocence to men like me. The canker has eaten too deep."

These words gave Freda a sudden chill, recalling to her unwilling mind the mysterious murder of Blewitt. She shuddered, but she did not draw away.

"Well," said Crispin brusquely, "if you are frightened you can go away. I'm not detaining you."

She looked up with a flushed face, full of sensitive feeling.

"I am sorry and sad with thinking of things which can't be undone," she said softly; "but I am not frightened."

He put his hand gently upon her head. She fancied that she heard him murmur: "God bless you." In a few moments, however, he withdrew his hand abruptly, and said that he must "be off."

"And you must go out of this place," he continued in his harder tone. "We don't allow intruders here, you know."

He led her up the stone staircase to the panel-door, which he unlocked. Then he helped her through into the gallery, and said "Good-night" in his usual matter-of-fact, brusque manner. But Freda was not to be repulsed. Before he could close the door, she caught his hand, and held it firmly, forcing him to listen to her.

"Crispin," she whispered, "remember what I said. John Thurley was kind to me. Don't let them hurt him. Promise."

But he would not promise. His face grew stern again, and he put her off with a laugh as he freed his hand.

"Don't worry yourself with silly fancies," he said shortly. "He's all right."

He closed the door sharply and fastened it. Freda remained for a few moments listening to his footsteps as he went down the stone stairs. Then remembering with excitement, that "Crispin" had forgotten to ask her how she got in, and that the way through the library into the locked-up portion of the house was still open, she went downstairs, and passed again through the door among the bookshelves.

She would try and get down to the scaur by the secret way the smugglers used.

CHAPTER XXIII.

FREDA went through the secret door the second time with more bravery then she had felt on the first occasion. For although she was bound on an expedition the dangers of which it was impossible to deny, she had now at least some knowledge of the risks she ran; and she was fortified by the belief that, even if she should not see him, her father would be about, within call perhaps, if she should run any danger from his rough associates. So she crept down into the room in which she had before hidden herself, very softly, listening as she went.

She could hear no sound. Her father had disappeared, leaving the light lowered. She crossed the floor almost on tip-toe, and peeped down through the opening. It was quite dark down there now; she could not even see the table round which the men had sat. She raised her head again and looked round her. She must go into that cellar, but she dared not go without a light. Becoming used to the silence, and feeling more secure, she began to make a tour of the room, hunting and groping very carefully. For, she thought, there must certainly be lanterns about somewhere; they would be a necessary part of a smuggler's stock-in-trade. And truly, when she did at last stumble upon the right quarters, she found a selection of lanterns which would have equipped the band twice over. They were stored in a corner-cupboard, and were of all shapes and sizes, some old, battered and useless, some new and untried. Freda made a careful choice, fitted her lantern with a candle which she found in a box on a shelf, and helped herself to a box of matches. Then she returned to the opening in the floor, threw down the rope-ladder, and began the descent.

To the lame girl, quite unaccustomed to adventures of this sort, this part of the journey was neither easy nor pleasant. Her trembling feet only found firm footing on each succeeding rung after much futile swinging to and fro, desperate clinging to the swaying ropes, and nervous fears that her protruding foot would be caught by a rough hand from below. But she reached the cellar-floor in safety, and proceeded to light her lantern. Then she took a survey of the room.

It was large, lofty, stone-walled, and very cold. There was an oil-stove in one corner, but it was not burning. There were no stores of tobacco or spirits kept here, only lumber of ship's gear, broken oars, coils of rope, some ends of rusty chain and such like. Freda, after a hasty inspection, proceeded to the corner where the men had disappeared. Here there was a large opening in the floor, from which a damp, earthy smell rose as she stooped to examine it. Freda could have no doubt that this was the entrance to a subterranean passage.

She drew back in horror which made her cold and wet from head to foot. Could she dare to trust herself alone in the very bowels of the earth, away from all hope of help if one of the rough and brutal men she had seen that evening should meet her?

She hesitated.

Then she thought of poor John Thurley, who had been so good to her: perhaps he was even then lying stunned or dead on the scaur, struck down by one of her father's servants in evil. Ashamed of her hesitation, fired with the determination to try to save him, she dropped on to her knees, covered her face with her hands, and prayed for strength and courage. Then she sprang up, boldly grasped her crutch in her right hand and her lantern in her left, and plunged into the passage with rapid steps.

There were a few worn stone steps to begin with, then a gentle slope, and then a long, straight run. The passage was narrow and walled with stones, old and green with damp. At frequent intervals air and daylight were let in through small iron gratings which seemed to be a very long way overhead. It was not difficult to breathe, and the passage being stoned-paved and drained, the way so far was smooth and easy. Freda did not know how long she had been down there nor how far she had gone, when she became aware that the ground was sloping up again. Then came a flight of steps upwards. At the top of these steps Freda found herself in a very small octagonal chamber, which contained part of a broken stone spiral staircase, going upwards. Behind this staircase there was another large hole in the ground.

Freda guessed that she must be on the ground-floor of one of the towers of the Abbey-church. In the wall in front of her was a stout wooden door, which was ajar. She pushed it softly, guessing from this circumstance that there must be some one about. Putting her head through the aperture, she saw that she was in the western tower of the north transept of the ruined church. She thought she heard a man's voice softly whistling to himself, but it did not sound very near, so she ventured to push the door open a little further and to slip through.

A clear, white moon, not long risen, was beginning to shine on the old pile, and to cast long lines of bright light and black shade between the old arches. To Freda the beautiful sight gave a fresh horror. How dared these men ply their wicked trade in the very shelter of these holy walls? She crept out, feeling more secure while she stood on this sacred ground, and treading with noiseless footsteps down the grass-grown nave, peeped through the broken window through which Robert Heritage had come to speak to her. She could trace in the moonlight the foot-path through the meadow outside to the outer wall, and beyond that she could just see a horse's ears, and a whip standing up in such a fashion as to convince her that it was in a cart. She waited without a sound while she heard the soft whistling nearer and nearer, and then, peeping through the loose stones, she saw stolid Josiah Kemm, walking slowly to and fro under the church walls, with his hands behind him. He saw her immediately, and started forward to find out who was watching him.

Freda was ready for him, however; the risks and excitement of the adventure had made her quick-witted. She drew herself from a crouching attitude to her full height, and said, in a clear voice:

"Is it you, Josiah Kemm?"

The man did not answer; he made a step back, taken by surprise. She continued:

"I think you must have heard of me. I am Captain Mulgrave's daughter."

He touched his hat rather surlily, and seemed restless, as if uncertain what she knew, or how he ought to treat her.

"Why are you not waiting in the court-yard?" she asked with an inspiration. "You take your cart in there generally, don't you?"

She thought that if she could persuade him that she knew all about his business, she could perhaps learn from him by what way she could get down to the scaur. Her confident tone had the desired effect. After a few minutes' hesitation, during which Freda pretended to be unconcerned, but felt sick with anxiety, he answered:

"Well, noa; generally is a big word. Ah do soometoimes go into t' yard, but more often Ah weait here." He paused, but as his hearer took care to show no deep interest, he presently went on: "Ye see, it depends whether Ah teake t' stuff streight from t' boat, or whether Ah have to teake what's stored in t' Abbey."

"I see. If you take what is stored up, the cart waits under the gallery window in the courtyard."

"Aye. An' Crispin Bean brings oop t' stuff, an' thraws it aht."

"While if you take it straight from the boat——?"

"Why, Ah weait here, and when they've hauled it oop t' cliff and brought it along t' first passage, they bring it oop to me, instead o' teaking it along t' other passage into t' Abbey."

"Aren't you afraid of people passing late, who might see your cart and wonder why it was so often standing there?"

Kemm shook his head decidedly, with a dry laugh.

"Noa, missie. T' fowk hereabout's all on our soide."

"Oh," said Freda.

She was wondering now how she should make her escape and find the second passage; that which, by Kemm's account, led down to the beach. He himself unwittingly came to her succour.

"Ah thowt Ah heerd summat!" he suddenly exclaimed.

He gave a low, long whistle, but there was no reply. So without heeding Freda, who had succeeded in making him believe that she was in the secrets of the gang, he got through the ruined window, and went to the tower in the north transept. Freda hopped after him as quickly as she could. He pushed open the door, and going to the hole under the broken staircase, called down it, and whistled. There was no answering sound.

"False alarm!" said he, as he stepped again out into the transept.

But Freda had disappeared. She had followed him into the tower, and having blown out her lantern, crouched on the lowest stair until she found herself alone again. Then, waiting until Kemm's voice, still calling to her, sounded a long way off, she relighted her candle, ran to the hole, and seeing a ladder in it, went down without delay. The underground passage into which this led her was very different from that which led from the church to the Abbey-house. As a matter of fact, the latter was of very ancient origin, having been carefully built and paved, six hundred years ago, as a private way for the Abbot between his house and the church. The passage which led from the church to the cliff, however, was an entirely modern and base imitation, dug and cut roughly out of the red clay and hard rock of which the cliffs were composed, ill-drained, ill-ventilated, almost impassable here and there through the slipping of great masses of the soft red clay. From time to time Freda, hurrying and stumbling along as best she could, now ankle-deep in sticky mud, now hurting her feet against loose stones, saw a faint gleam of moonlight above her, let in, as in the other passage, through a narrow grating, which would pass on the surface of the ground for the entrance to a drain. At last the passage widened suddenly, and she found herself in a low-roofed cave, partly natural, partly artificial, with a narrow opening, not looking straight out to sea, but towards a jutting point of the cliff.

Here Freda paused for a moment, afraid that some one might start up from one of the dark corners. But the total silence reassured her. There was a lantern hanging on the rough wall, and there was a bench on which lay some clothes. On the floor a few planks had been laid down side by side, with a worn and damp straw mat, evidently used for removing from the boots of the gang the clay collected on the way through the passage.

But the most noteworthy objects in the cave were a strong iron bar which was fixed from rock to rock across the mouth, to which a rope ladder was fastened, which hung down the surface of the cliff, and a windlass fastened firmly in the ground, by which, as Freda guessed, bales of smuggled tobacco and kegs of contraband spirit, were hauled up from the scaur below. She crept to the entrance and peeped out.

The moon was not yet fully risen, but there was light enough for the girl to make out the admirable position of this den above the water. Not only was the opening invisible from the sea, except for a little space close in shore where even small boats scarcely ventured, but it was also hidden from any one on the rocky beach below or on the cliff above by jutting points of rock; while a perpendicular slab of rock, descending sheer to the scaur beneath it, made it quite inaccessible from below except by the means the smugglers used.

After waiting a few minutes, and peering down on to the rocks below without hearing the least sound except the splash of the incoming tide, Freda resolved to descend, and take her chance of being seen. She must find out if John Thurley was there, and if any harm had come to him.

CHAPTER XXIV.

AT the very first step she made on the rope ladder, Freda sustained a sudden shock which almost caused her to lose her grip of the ropes. With a wild, wailing cry, a great sea-gull flew out from a cleft in the rock a few feet from her, and almost touching her with its long grey-white wings, flew past her and circled in the air below, still keeping up its melancholy cry of alarm or warning, which was taken up by a host of its companions. Although she had heard the shrill sea-bird's cry before, it had never sounded so lugubrious as now. The beating of the advancing tide on the rocks below made a mournful accompaniment to the bird's wailing; and Freda, startled and alarmed, clung tremblingly to the ladder, not daring to descend a single step, as she felt the rush of air fanned by their long wings, and dreaded lest the great birds should attack her. At last, one by one, they circled lower and lower, until they reached the sea, and, folding their wings, settled in a flock upon the water: not till then did the girl venture to proceed on her journey.

This descent, though long, was much less difficult than her first trial of a rope-ladder in the secret-room of the Abbey; for the ladder was firmly fixed to a rock below into which two iron hooks had been driven. The greatest danger she had to contend with during the descent was the extreme cold, which benumbed her fingers, and made it scarcely possible for her to grasp the ropes, and to hold her crutch at the same time; the lantern she had extinguished and tied round her waist. At last her feet touched the solid rock: she drew a long breath of relief: she had reached the scaur. Turning slowly, she took a survey of the spot.

The cliff frowned at an immense height above her, rugged, and steep as a wall. She was standing on a narrow ledge formed of broken bits of rock which had, from time to time, been detached from the main cliff by force of water and rough weather. Only a few feet away the sea was breaking into little foaming cascades against the boulders. At sea, just out of the silver light cast by the moon, and some distance away from shore, she could dimly see a boat, which she guessed to be her father's yacht. On the right hand, a jutting point of cliff shut out the view; on the left a bend in the cliff formed a tiny bay, beyond which a sort of rough pier of black rocks stretched out into the sea.

The bay was the point the smugglers would make for, she felt sure; it was in this direction, then, that she must go. She dared not light her lantern, but had to trust to the faint light of the moon. The way was infinitely more difficult than she had expected: to scramble, to crawl, sometimes to leap from rock to rock would have made the path a hard one for anybody; to a girl with a crutch it was absolutely dangerous. Panting, bruised, breathless, she at last scrambled over the last rough stone and found, to her relief, that in the tiny bay there was a stretch of smooth land, part clay, part sand, which had gathered in this inlet at the foot of the cliff, and on which a short, coarse grass grew. This seemed a paradise to Freda after her exertion: she sank down and rested her limbs, which were trembling with fatigue.

After a few moments, however, her sense of relief and rest was broken by a sensation of horror, which seemed to creep up her tired limbs and settle like a pall upon her. The utter silence, which not even a sea-gull now broke; the great wall of rock stretching round her, like a giant arm pointing its finger out to sea; the solitude, and the piercing cold all united to impress the girl with a dread of what she might be going to see and hear. With a little sobbing cry she shivered and shut out the scene by burying her face in her hands.

Suddenly a faint sound caused her to start up; it was the splash of oars in the water. There was a fringe of rock between the smooth land and the sea, under cover of which Freda ran, stumbling as she went, in the direction of the rough natural pier. From this she thought she would be able to get a clear view of all that went on by sea or by land. But on nearer approach this natural pier proved to be much more difficult of access than she had supposed; for it consisted of a huge rock, flattened on the top, rising so high out of the water that it would need a climb to get upon it. Still Freda resolved to try to overcome the difficulty. At this point she suddenly came in full view of the approaching boat, which was making straight for the beach. In another moment she had begun the climb. She had scarcely got her head above the level of the top of the rock, when she caught sight of a man crouching down on the smooth wave-worn surface, watching the approach of the boat with eagerness which betrayed itself in his very attitude. It was John Thurley.

Startled by the sight, Freda lost the footing she had obtained on the flaky, rotten side of the rock, and slipping back a few steps, found that she had all her work to do over again.

But she was quicker this time, her experience having stood her in good stead. In a very few moments she had won back the lost ground, and again glanced up at the crouching figure. She had scarcely done so when she saw, and yet hardly believed that she saw, a second figure crossing the smooth surface of the rock in the direction of the first, crossing stealthily, with the cat-like tread she knew so well.

It was the man who had said he would "be on the watch."

She wanted to cry out, she tried to cry out, but only a hoarse rattle came forth from her parched throat. She knew what was going to happen, though she saw no weapon in the rascal's hand; and the knowledge paralysed her. Before she could draw breath the blow had fallen: with a horrible cry John Thurley sprang up with a backward step, turned, staggered, and fell in a dark heap on the rock at his assailant's feet.

Freda's voice had come back now; but it was too late. She stifled back her cries, got up, by digging heels and clawing fingers, somehow, anyhow, on to the top of the rock, and skimming along the surface, lame as she was, like a bird, came up with the man who had threatened her that evening. He started, looking up at her with blood-shot, evil eyes, as she laid her hand upon his arm.

"Hands off, missus," said he roughly, assuming more coarseness of accent than usual.

"No," answered the girl fiercely, as she fastened her fingers with a firmer grip on his arm, "you have exceeded your orders to-night, and now you've got to obey mine. You have to help me carry that man you have hurt into the house, into the Abbey."

The man was impressed, in spite of himself, by her manner.

"He's dead," he said impatiently. "Haven't you had enough corpses about the place lately?"

"He is not dead; he is moving; and you will take him in, dead or alive. Do you forget I am your master's daughter?"

"Perhaps I'm my master's master," said he shortly. Then, with a sudden access of fury, to which his potations of earlier in the evening evidently gave reckless intensity, he suddenly held up, with a threatening movement, the knife with which he had stabbed his victim. It was red with blood—a sickening sight. But Freda was too much excited and exasperated to show a sign of fear now.

"You dare not hurt me," she cried, in her high, girlish voice, that echoed among the cliffs. "If this poor man dies you may escape; but if you kill *me*, my father will not let you live another day."

She thought it was her words which suddenly caused him to drop from a defiant into a cringing attitude, and to hold himself quite limply and meekly under her grasp. But his shifting glances made her turn her head, and she saw that her father was standing behind, with his eyes fixed on the fallen man. Freda forgot her reticence, forgot his cautions. Rushing towards him with her left hand outstretched, she cried, with a break in her voice:

"Father! father!"

He did not rebuke her. Taking a step forward, he caught the girl in his arms, and looked tenderly down into her white face.

"What business have you here?" he said, but without harshness.

"I came to save John Thurley," she answered, trembling. "But I was too late. Make this man take him home—father—to the Abbey."

He shook his head, while the other man gave a short laugh.

"He's done for, guv'nor," said he curtly. "Sorry if I went too far, but it's always dangerous work to put your nose into other people's business."

Freda was on her knees beside the fallen man.

"He's alive," she cried triumphantly. "Make haste, oh, make haste, and we shall be able to save him!"

"Him? Yes," said her father gruffly and dubiously. "But how about ourselves? His safety is our danger, child; don't you understand?"

"But, father, you wouldn't have him *murdered*! Oh, if it is true you care for me—and you do, you do—tell that man to help you; and take him in! Do this for me, as you would have done it for my mother."

Captain Mulgrave hesitated. Then he tried to speak in a peremptory and angry voice, but broke down. Turning at last sharply to the assailant, who had been watching him with hungry intentness, he made a gesture towards the wounded man.

"Here, Crispin, help me—to take him in. We must obey the ladies," he said with a hoarse and almost tremulous attempt at levity.

The grin died out of the lean and withered face, and Freda caught upon it an expression of so much baulked malignity that she wondered whether succour at these unwilling hands would mean death to the succoured one. There was nothing for her to do but to watch, however, while her father, with a skilful hand, tore his own shirt into bandages, with which he stopped the flow of blood from the wounded man's side. Then, giving the word to start, he and his unwilling assistant lifted the still unconscious man and began the difficult journey to the Abbey.

CHAPTER XXV.

THE moon was high by the time Captain Mulgrave and his subordinate started for the Abbey with their unwelcome guest.

John Thurley was still unconscious as they lifted him from the rock; and the jolting to which they were forced to subject him, as they made the difficult descent to the level land, failed to rouse him to the least sign of life. Indeed Freda, who followed close, not without suspicions of foul play in one of the bearers, was afraid that this journey was a hopeless one, and that it was a dead man they would carry into the Abbey.

"Up the steps," directed Captain Mulgrave briefly.

And instead of turning to the left, towards the cave, they crossed the stretch of flat, grass-grown land in the direction of a rough flight of steps, partly cut in the cliff itself and partly formed of stones brought for the purpose, which, guarded on one side by a primitive handrail, formed the communication for the public between the top of the cliff and the scaur.

"It's a long way round, guv'nor," grumbled the other. "Better haul him up our way with the rest of the stuff."

Freda uttered an angry and impatient exclamation. Her father who, to her horror, had appeared not unwilling to act on the suggestion, now shook his head and again nodded towards the steps. The other, though he had to submit to the directions of his chief, did so with a very bad grace, and muttered many expressions of ill-will as he staggered along under his share of the burden. For the unfortunate John Thurley was a solidly built, heavy man, and the ascent up the face of the cliff was not an easy one even in ordinary circumstances.

When they had at last, after many pauses, reached the top of the cliff, the little wizened face puckered up again with an expression of intense slyness.

"The boys won't be able to get on without one or other of us, guv'nor," he suggested. "They'll have got the stuff through to the house by this time, and if there 's nobody there to look after them they'll just get roaring drunk, and perhaps manage to get up from the cellar for more liquor, and kick up no end of a disturbance."

Freda, who was afraid her father might leave her alone with this odious man and the unconscious Thurley, instantly struck in with a suggestion.

"There's Josiah Kemm waiting about by the ruin," she said. "I suppose you have some whistle or signal that he would know, and he would bring his cart."

She would have suggested going in search of him herself, but she could not pretend to have enough confidence in her companions for that. Her father smiled, and seemed to be both amused and pleased by her quickness. The other man, however, openly scowled at her. After a few moments' consideration, Captain Mulgrave turned to his subordinate.

"You whistle," he ordered shortly. "When Kemm comes, she" (nodding towards Freda) "will tell him what to do."

So saying, he turned, and descending a dozen steps below the top of the cliff, concealed himself; while the other man, most unwillingly, whistled four times. By this Freda concluded that the fact of Captain Mulgrave's being still alive was unknown to some members at least of the gang acting under him.

She knelt down by the wounded man, and was frightened by the coldness of his face and hands, and by the impossibility of discovering whether he still breathed. In a very few moments she was relieved to hear the rattle of wheels; and almost immediately afterwards the cart appeared in sight, and stopped in the road at the nearest point to where the wounded man was lying. There was a gate in the wall, and she could see Josiah Kemm opening it.

"Bring the cart through," she cried out shrilly. "The cart!"

Kemm stopped, not at first understanding.

"T' cart!" he echoed wonderingly.

"Yes, yes. Say yes," she continued, turning with an impetuous air of command to her companion. He repeated sullenly:

"Yes, bring the cart."

Kemm obeyed. But his disappointment, disgust and dismay were unbounded when, instead of a few bales of smuggled tobacco, he found that his cart was wanted to bear the wounded man. His superstitious fears were aroused, and he drew back hastily.

"He's dead!" he muttered, "yon chap's dead. It's onlucky to carry a dead mon."

But Freda besought him, coaxed, persuaded, promised until the stubborn Yorkshireman, impressed by her imperious manner, began to think that in obeying her, he was currying favour with the higher powers. So that at last he stooped, hoisted up the unfortunate man, placed him in his cart, lifted Freda herself into the front seat without waiting to be asked, and turned his horse's head, by her direction, towards the Abbey.

Freda was trembling with triumph, but also with some apprehension. The Abbey was the only place to which she could take the wounded man, and yet she could not but fear that it might prove a very unsafe refuge. The little grinning man, whom they had left behind on the edge of the cliff, was a trusted person in her father's mysterious house, and could go and come by secret ways, whenever he pleased. Her only hope lay with Mrs. Bean. Freda believed in the little woman's real kindness of heart, and then too she would get at her first, before the housekeeper could be influenced by less honest counsels.

The cart with its occupants reached the Abbey-lodge in very few minutes. At the inner gate there was a little longer delay, and then Mrs. Bean appeared and let them in without question.

"I didn't expect you to-night, Mr. Kemm," was all she said.

But she started back in astonishment and dismay when he said:

"Ah've browt ye back a friend an' a stranger, Mrs. Bean. One's a leady, an' t'other's a gen'leman."

At the same moment Freda, who had got down with Kemm's help, ran up and put her arm round Nell's neck.

"Mrs. Bean, dear Mrs. Bean," she whispered, "it's a friend of mine, the gentleman you saw me with at the churchyard, and he's very, very ill. You'll be kind to him, won't you?"

But Nell was not at all sure about that. She even began by resolutely refusing to allow him to be brought into the house. Kemm, however, as resolutely refused to take him away again. At last Freda thought of away of overcoming the housekeeper's objections.

"It was my father himself who brought him up from the scaur," she whispered, in a voice too low for Kemm to hear. And as the housekeeper looked at her incredulously, she added: "My father, the man I have always called Crispin. He told me to bring him home."

Mrs. Bean turned abruptly to Kemm.

"Where did you find this gentleman?" she asked. "Who was with him?"

"This little leady, and your husband."

Freda started. The wizened and grinning man who had threatened her and stabbed John Thurley was, then, Nell's husband, the veritable Crispin Bean.

Kemm's answer, while it disturbed her, reassured the housekeeper, who reluctantly gave Kemm permission to bring the unconscious man indoors.

"I'm sure I don't know where to put him," she said discontentedly, though Freda was happy in discovering a gleam of pity in her round face.

"Put him in my father's room," said Freda with unexpected authority. And she led the way upstairs, beckoning to Kemm to follow her with his burden. She had rapidly decided that this room would be the safest in the house.

As soon as John Thurley had been placed upon the bed and Kemm had gone, Freda was delighted to find that her trust in Nell's goodness of heart had not been misplaced. The young girl wanted to go for a doctor, but this the housekeeper would not allow, saying that she could do what had to be done as well as any man. She proceeded to prove this by binding up his wound with skilful hands. Presently John Thurley opened his eyes, as he had done several times during the journey from the beach. This time, however, he was not allowed to relapse into unconsciousness. Applying a restorative to his lips, Mrs. Bean spoke to him cheerfully, and got some sort of feebly muttered answer. He caught sight of Freda, who was helping Mrs. Bean, and gave her a smile of recognition. But Nell sent her away lest he should want to talk to her.

Freda left the room obediently, but went no further away than the great window-seat on the landing outside. Here she curled herself up, trying to keep warm, and looked out on the moonlit stretch of country. She was full of disquieting thoughts. This man, who had been kind to her, whose life she was trying to save, had seen the murderer of the man-servant Blewitt, and could recognise him. The fact of his having kept this knowledge to himself for so long could only be explained by his belief that the murderer was dead, and could not be brought to justice. If he were to learn that the murderer was not dead after all, Freda felt that she knew the man well enough to be sure that no consideration would deter him from bringing punishment upon the criminal. And that criminal she could no longer doubt was her father. If she could only see her father again, and warn him to keep away, as she had meant but had missed the opportunity to do, it would be all right. It never occurred to her that her influence with John Thurley would be strong enough to induce him to keep silence. On the other hand, there was danger to be feared from the real Crispin; perhaps also from his wife, who, when she learnt who struck the blow, might be too dutiful to her husband to continue her care of his victim. But in this she did Nell an injustice.

While the girl was still sitting in the window-seat crouching in an attitude of deep depression, the door of her father's room softly opened, and Nell came up to her. She looked worried but spoke very gently.

"This is a bad business," she began. "It's one of my lord and master's tricks, no doubt. And the worst of it is that when Crispin takes a job like this on hand, he doesn't generally stop till he's finished it."

"But can't you prevent him? Can't you persuade him that he's hurt this poor man enough?" asked Freda anxiously.

Nell shook her head.

"My dear," said she, "since you've found out so much you may as well know the rest. Crispin's a bad man, but a moderately good husband. If I were to interfere with him in any way, he would not be at all a better man, and he'd be a much worse husband. Those are the terms we live upon: I hold my tongue to him, and he holds his to me."

"Then you won't take care of this poor man any longer?"

"Yes, I will as long as I can. What he will most want is—watching. You understand?"

"Yes," said Freda, trembling.

"The wound isn't dangerous, I think if he's kept quiet. And I'm used to nursing. Who is he?"

Freda hesitated. But the truth could not be concealed from Nell much longer, so at last she faltered:

"He is sent down—by the government—to look after the smuggling."

The housekeeper's face changed, as if a warrant of death had been contained in those words.

"The Lord help him then!" was all she said.

But Freda was so horror-struck at her tone that she sprang up and ran like a hare to the door of the sick man's room.

"What are you going to do?" asked Nell.

"I don't know," sobbed Freda. "But—but I think I ought to put him on his guard."

"No," said Nell peremptorily. "Don't disturb him now. Come here with me; I have something to tell you."

Fancying from the housekeeper's manner that an idea for helping John Thurley had occurred to her, Freda allowed herself to be led away to the disused room opposite.

CHAPTER XXVI.

BEFORE the two women had entered the musty, damp-smelling apartment which had once been one of the best bedrooms of the house, the younger began to feel that her companion was unnerved and unstrung. Indeed they were no sooner inside than Mrs. Bean, sinking down on a chair, burst into tears. This was such an unusual sign of weakness in the self-contained housekeeper, that Freda, in alarm, stood for a few moments quite helpless, not knowing what to do. But the kindly womanliness of her nature soon prompted the right action, and putting her arms round Nell's neck, she clung to her and soothed her with few words but with genuine tenderness.

Recovering herself, Nell suddenly pushed her away.

"It is not fit that I should sit here and be comforted by you, child," she said, abruptly but not harshly, "when it's you have brought it all upon us—and it's ruin, that's what it is—ruin!"

"Mrs. Bean! What do you mean?"

"Why, that this is the end of it all, the end I've been dreading for years, but worse, a thousand times worse, than I ever guessed it would be! I thought it would only be the smuggling, and a break-up of the old gang. I never thought it would be murder!"

"Murder!" hissed out Freda, not indeed in surprise, but in fear.

"Yes, and you know it, for all you may say. You know that the man-servant Blewitt was murdered. And if you go in there, and listen to that man's mutterings"—and she pointed towards the sick-room—"you'll know more."

Freda shook from head to foot, and at first tried in vain to speak.

"What does *he* say! What does he know?"

"He knows that it was murder, for one thing, but he knows more than that, or I'm much mistaken. It's on his mind, and as the fever rises, it will all come out."

She began to sob again and to dry her eyes. Freda at first stood motionless beside her, but as Nell got the better of her outburst, the girl took courage and touched her on the shoulder.

"Mrs. Bean," she said in a hoarse whisper, "who do you think did it?"

There was no answer.

"Do you think it was—Crispin?"

She asked this question timidly, but Nell did not seem offended by the suggestion. She shook her head, however.

"No, he was in the house here with me. He had been out all night in the yacht, and he was lying down to have a nap on the sofa in my sitting-room. Then"—she lowered her voice, and spoke in an awe-struck whisper—"the master came in, looking white and—and queer, bloodshot about the eyes and that, and he called Crispin out, and they both left the house together, by the back way, through the garden. And I wondered, and watched, and presently I saw them come back and they were carrying something. I didn't guess what sort of burden it was though, not then. But while I was watching, your ring came at the bell; and as I was crossing the yard to answer it Captain Mulgrave came running after me, and he said: 'If it's my daughter, say I've shot myself, for I'm going away to-night, and I don't mean to meet her.'"

Here Freda interrupted, in some distress:

"He didn't mean to meet me! Didn't he want me to come, then?"

"Yes, and no, I think. I believe it made him feel ashamed of himself; it reminded him, perhaps, of old days when your mother was alive, and made him feel sorry that things were not with him now as they were then."

Freda, with tears in her eyes, drew nearer to Nell as the latter made these tardy confessions.

"Mind," continued the housekeeper, drawing back suddenly as the girl's arm stole round her neck, "it's only like guess-work what I'm telling you. The Captain has never said anything of the sort to me——"

"But it's *true*!" whispered Freda eagerly, "it's true: I know it, I feel it. Go on, go on."

"Well, at any rate that was only part of what he felt, remember; for he's done things he had better have left undone for a good many years now. He also felt that a girl would be in the way here with her prying eyes—as it has proved; and between the wish to see you and the wish not to see you, he was quite unmanned. In fact, he's not been the same man since you've been about: it's Crispin who has become master."

Nell said this with sorrow rather than with pride. She paused, and Freda urged her to go on:

"And on that day, when you were coming to let me in——?" she suggested.

"Ah, yes. Suddenly he made up his mind to let you in himself, and he said: 'Don't let her know who I am; I shan't.' '*I* shan't say anything, sir, you may be sure,' I said. And with that I walked back to my kitchen, and he let you in, and you took him for Crispin, as you know. And ever since then he's been in two minds, now making believe to be dead, so that he might get away quietly, and now bent on staying here, whatever happened."

"Whatever happened!" repeated Freda. "Why, what should happen, Mrs. Bean?"

The housekeeper rose, and made answer very abruptly:

"I suppose you have some nerve, or you wouldn't have got down on the scaur by yourself to-night! Well, come with me, then."

She opened the door, and led the girl back to the sick-room, where John Thurley lay quietly enough, looking up at the old-fashioned bed-draperies, and muttering to himself in a low voice from time to time. Leaving Freda by the door, with a significant sign to be silent, Nell went up to the bedside, and put her hand on the sick man's forehead.

"Are you better now?" she asked gently.

"Better!" he muttered in a husky voice. "I don't know. I haven't time to think about that."

"Why, what's troubling you?"

"Oh, you know, you know. The old thing."

"What, these men?"

"Yes, the gang. They've got to be caught, you know, to be caught, every man Jack of them."

"Why, what have they done?"

He went on muttering to himself, and she had to repeat the question.

"Done! They've done everything: robbed, cheated, killed."

Freda started.

"Hush, hush, sir. You are going too far, aren't you?"

"Too far, yes, he went too far—that morning," said the sick man drowsily, "I saw him slinking about—and I saw him take out his revolver—and he crept up past me, over the snow, to the top of the hill."

"But you didn't see him shoot, sir, now did you?"

He shook his head.

"I saw him return—presently, without the revolver," he went on in a very low voice, "with a look on his face—all the savagery gone out of it—I did not understand it."

"But when you heard later that a man had disappeared, and then a rumour that he had been murdered——?"

"I knew that I had seen the murderer. I knew his face. It was he."

He uttered these last words slowly and dreamily, and then as Nell asked no more questions, he subsided into silence, and stared again at the bed-hangings. Freda slipped softly out of the room, ran downstairs into the library as fast as her feet and her crutch could take her, and went through the bookshelf door into the secret portion of the house for the third time that night. If she could only find her father, and warn him! That was the thought that was in her mind as she tripped up the first narrow stone staircase and down the second, and reached the room where she had had her interview with him.

There was no one either in this apartment or in the cellar below. The rope-ladder was hanging down just as she had left it, the lamp was still burning. Would her father come in by this way, she wondered, as she crouched on the floor by the opening, and listened for the sound of footsteps approaching from below. At first she heard nothing. She dared not go down into the cellar again, for fear of meeting Crispin, who bore no goodwill either to her or to the patient she had introduced into the house. Presently a distant rumbling down in the earth below riveted her attention. It grew louder and nearer until there was no mistaking the fact that some one was coming up the underground passage.

It was not until that moment that Freda realised the danger of her situation. She had been reckoning on meeting her father. But what foundation had she for this hope? She had scarcely acknowledged to herself that she had very little, when she perceived that her worst fears were fulfilled, and that the man who, lantern in hand, had just reached the floor of the cellar, was the real Crispin Bean. The faint cry which escaped her lips attracted his attention, and with an oath on his lips and a scowl on his face he made a rush for the ladder.

Freda was too quick for him. She pulled it up out of his reach with a jerk, flung to the trap-door which closed the opening, and with some difficulty drew the heavy iron bolt which made it fast. Then, frightened both by what she had done, and by the storm of oaths and blasphemies to which Crispin gave free vent, she crept out of the room like a mouse, and gained the library as fast as she could.

CHAPTER XXVII.

DANGER had roused Freda from a little frightened girl into a ready-witted and daring woman. No sooner had she fastened down the trap-door and made it impossible for Crispin to get into the house from below than another idea for securing the safety of her sick guest flashed into her mind. As soon as the thought suggested itself, she set about carrying it out. Flying out of the house, across the court-yard, unlocking the first gate and taking care to keep it from closing by a stone at its base, she was out of breath by the time she reached the lodge-gates and pulled lustily at the bell. Of course the old woman was asleep, and it was some moments before the gates opened. In the meantime, Freda had had another inspiration. As soon as one of the gates opened, she slipped through, and placed a stone at the foot as she had done with the inner gate, and watched for the effect. As she had hoped when the spring was pulled again by the lodgekeeper from within, the gate swung to, but remained open a couple of inches. Satisfied, the young girl went on her way.

She crossed the churchyard, not without certain nervous and superstitious terrors, for some of which her convent training was perhaps responsible: and passing by the shapeless church with its squat stone tower, and the seat underneath where the old fishermen would sit and smoke their pipes and tell their yarns, with one eye on the listener, and one on their old love, the sea, she came to the steep flight of worn stone steps that led down into the town.

The moon was in her second quarter, and the light she gave was bright enough for Freda to see the silver river below, for the tide was high. Here and there the weak little town-lights twinkled, but they were so far between that they did not save Freda from a feeling that she was plunging into an abyss of blackness and horror, as she found herself in the steep, stone-paved street at the bottom of the steps. She had been told where the Vicarage was, knew that she must turn to the left, and go down Church Street until she came to it. But the sound of her footsteps and her crutch on the rough stones of the narrow street frightened her. The little irregular, old-fashioned shops, with their overhanging eaves and tiny windows, seemed to the scared girl to have a threatening aspect; she fancied every moment that one of the desperate characters with whom her imagination peopled them was lying in wait for her at the entrance of one of the squalid courts which ran between the houses. Past the tiny market-place she ran, with a frightened glance at the pillars which supported a pretentious town-hall about the size of a large beehive. But no one was in hiding among them; and she reached the Vicarage without even meeting a drunken fisherman finishing his evening's enjoyment by a nap on a friend's doorstep.

Her ring at the bell brought Mrs. Staynes to an upper window, and a few words of entreaty brought her to the front door. The sight of Miss Mulgrave without hat or cloak at three o'clock in the morning filled her with shocked amazement; but when Freda implored her to come with her at once to help to nurse a sick man, a stranger, who had been wounded on the scaur that night in some not very clearly explained manner, the good little woman at once agreed to come, and retreated to get ready. Her toilette being always of the simplest, she soon reappeared, tying on her rusty mushroom hat and clasping round her neck a circular cloak, the rabbit-skin lining of which had been so well worn that there was only enough of the fur left to come off on the garments it touched. But to Freda's eyes, who saw in her coming safety for John Thurley, no princess's court dress ever looked more pleasing than the ragged garments of the Vicar's old wife, as she stepped cheerfully out in the raw April morning, first insisting on tying up the young girl's head and shoulders in her garden shawl.

"You have sent for a doctor, my dear, of course?" she said.

"No," said Freda. "Mrs. Bean says it's nursing and watching he wants. So I thought of you. I knew you were good to the sick. Everybody says so."

"Everybody" only did the odd little woman justice. Tied to a selfish husband for whom she thought it an honour to slave, she had learned to look upon herself as born to drudge for his comfort and glory; and feeling that whatever she did as the Vicar's wife redounded to the Vicar's credit, she was a devoted nurse and visitor to the sick, at the disposal of anybody in the parish. She received Freda's thanks almost apologetically.

"It is a luxury to do good," she said.

And although her tone was dogmatic and "preaching," she meant what she said.

Nowhere could Freda have found a person better able to get her out of her difficulty. Even Mrs. Bean gave a sigh of relief, after the first moment of dismay at this unexpected intrusion of a stranger, on finding the burden of her responsibility thus suddenly lightened. Crispin would never dare do further harm to John Thurley while this "outsider" was about. The very personality of the quiet, chirpingly cheerful middle-aged woman, with her conversation largely made up of texts and quotations from the book of Common Prayer, her placid commonplaces, and her prosaic disbelief in any occurrence out of the common was healing and healthful to these two women who had been living under a volcano of crime and dread. When John Thurley raved in her presence of smuggling and murder, the little lady placidly ascribed his utterances to the effects of injudicious reading; when she heard a mysterious noise in the night which the other watchers knew too well how to account for, no arguments would have been strong enough to shake her conviction that it was caused by rats behind the wainscotting.

She brought in her train another safeguard for the sick man; the Reverend Berkeley, who missed his wife's ministrations on the one hand, but was delighted at the opportunity of rummaging in the old house on the other, was constant in his visits; so that under this pastoral surveillance no bodily harm to the sick man could be attempted; and Crispin, who, to Freda's horror, still lurked about the house, dared not show his face except to his wife.

John Thurley recovered rapidly; Mrs. Staynes soon gave up her watching for occasional visits, and indeed there seemed no reason why he should not go about his business. He must have been dull too, one would have thought; for Freda, when he came downstairs, avoided him as much as possible, dreading the fatal knowledge he possessed. She had never, since that eventful night on the scaur, been able to meet her father again, to warn him to keep out of the way of his danger. Every night now she hid herself in the secret portion of the house, watching and waiting for him. But he never came. Every day she would go out to the cliff's edge, looking out for the yacht; and then she would roam about the Abbey ruins, and listen at the door of the tower in the north transept, hoping to hear his voice or his tread. It was all in vain.

At last one day, when Thurley had been downstairs nearly a week, he met her flying through one of the passages, and asked if she would speak with him.

"I will only keep you a few minutes," he said humbly, apologetically. "I am going away. I must go away."

Freda began to tremble. She dreaded some revelation about her father, and felt that she must have a little while to prepare herself for what she might have to hear, and for the entreaties she must make.

"I—I have got to go and help Mrs. Bean now," she said in a frightened voice. "Won't it do this afternoon? I mean——"

She blushed and stammered, afraid that she seemed rude; but John Thurley answered at once eagerly:

"This afternoon will do perfectly."

Freda spent the intervening hours partly in prayer, partly in trying to devise entreaties which would move him to spare her father. In order to put off the evil hour of the interview, she roamed about the ruined church, supposing that Thurley was where he usually spent his time, in the library. Habit took her to the transept tower. She had not, this time, her usual thought of trying to meet her father; it was through custom, rather than by intention, that she leaned against the wooden door. To her surprise, it gave way, and she only just missed falling on her back. She forgot all about John Thurley in her excitement. This was only the second time she had found the door open, and she was convinced that there must be some one about. She listened at the opening, first of the one underground passage and then of the other, but could hear no sound in either. Should she dare to go down into the one which led to the cliff?

While she was hesitating, she was startled by a faint noise from outside the tower. It was like the falling of stones. At the same moment there was a sound of footsteps in the passage beneath her feet. She had to make up her mind quickly what she should do; and deciding that it would be less dangerous to meet an enemy outside the tower than in, if the new-comer should prove an enemy, she passed quickly into the church, and came face to face with John Thurley.

Her cheeks blanched, and she stood before him without a word to say. He, on his side, struck by the terror on her face, muttered an apology, and was turning to retreat, when a footstep in the tower caused him to stop. Freda recognised the tread, and a low cry escaped her.

"Go, go," she entreated in a hoarse voice. "Why do you stay when I beg you, implore you to go?"

John Thurley hesitated. But that moment's delay was too long. For the door of the tower was pulled roughly open, and Captain Mulgrave, who had heard his daughter's pleading appeared, bristling with anger, as her champion.

"Who is this annoying you?" he asked fiercely.

But Freda drew a long breath and said nothing. For the men had caught sight of each other, had exchanged a long, steady look. It was impossible to doubt that it was a recognition.

Captain Mulgrave did not repeat his question, asked for no further explanation. With a stare of quiet defiance he took a great key from his pocket, locked the door in the tower, and whistling to himself with a splendid affectation of unconcern, walked past his daughter and Thurley, and made his way over the fields towards the side-gate of Sea-Mew Abbey.

CHAPTER XXVIII.

FREDA watched her father's retreating figure for some moments, without daring to look at John Thurley's face. When at last she found the courage to throw a shy, frightened glance in his direction, she saw on his countenance an expression of deep pain and surprise as he gazed steadily at Captain Mulgrave.

"It is—my father," she faltered out, in pleading tones, while her great brown eyes were full of entreaty.

"I know, I know," he answered hastily, without looking at her.

And he began to pace up and down the choir, with his eyes on the long rough grass at his feet, and his hands behind his back. Freda felt the very faint hope she had entertained of moving him by her entreaties melt utterly away as she watched him. The whole face of the man—the steadfast eyes, square jaw, resolute mouth—all indicated strength of purpose, and a will difficult to turn. The trouble and anxiety which now clouded his face gave it no gentler character, but rather added sternness. After considering him in silence for a few minutes, during which he seemed intent on his own thoughts even to forgetfulness of her presence, she stole away down the nave, and getting through the window to the north side of the church, crossed the meadow towards the road.

As she approached the wall which separated the meadow from the road, Freda was startled by a man who sprang up suddenly on the other side. Already unstrung by the events of the preceding twenty minutes, she could scarcely repress a cry of alarm. The man, who had evidently expected some one else, touched his hat and said:

"Beg pardon, miss. Sorry if I frightened you. I was expecting to meet a friend here by appointment. I am afraid I startled you."

Freda wondered who he was. Already she knew enough of the Yorkshire types and the Yorkshire accent to be sure that he was not a native of this part of the country; and there was a sort of trimness and smartness about him in spite of the rough suit of clothes he wore, and a precision in his manner, which made her think he was some sort of official. She wondered whether it was John Thurley he was waiting for, and if so, what his business with him was.

Going back to the ruins, she had got into the shadow of the east end when she again came face to face with Thurley. The expression of his countenance had changed; instead of the frown of anxiety he had worn a few minutes before, care of another kind, far less stern, but scarcely less disquieting to the young girl, was stamped upon his somewhat rough features. Yet she could not have explained the feeling which caused her to start and blush, and to hope that he would let her pass without speaking.

But that was far from being his intention. He started forward at sight of her, and his face flushed.

"Ah, I was looking for you; I have something to say to you."

He turned to walk beside her, but went a few paces without saying anything further. When they reached the angle of the ruin he stopped and, looking down upon her rather shyly, said abruptly:

"Give me your arm. We are friends enough for that, aren't we?"

Freda shyly complied, and they turned and walked back under the shadow of the eastern wall of the ancient church.

"You are not afraid of me, are you?"

"No-o."

"No-o! Why No-o? You are *not* afraid of me, you know you are not. Then why, lately, have you always avoided me?"

There was a long silence. Then Freda said, in a weak little voice:

"I expect you know."

"You think I know too much about—about certain very disagreeable occurrences?"

The girl answered by a long sob of terror. He patted her arm kindly:

"Come, come, my knowledge shall never hurt *you*, little one. That is what I wanted to tell you. At least, it's part of it." Another pause. "Don't you want to hear the rest?"

"No, I don't think I do."

"But you must. First, I want to tell you that I know who saved my life and had me brought to the Abbey that night when I was attacked by those ruffians——"

"Ruffians!" Freda turned upon him quickly. "There was only one. My father wasn't——"

She stopped, and drew a deep breath.

"I know, I know," said Thurley.

"It was he who ordered that you were to be brought here—to the house."

"I know all about that," said he quietly.

By his tone Freda knew that he must have heard more than at the time had seemed possible.

"And I know who nursed me——"

"Mrs. Staynes."

"And who watched over me——"

"Mrs. Bean."

"And took care that I should come to no harm, although she knew all the time that it would be better for those she cared about if I did come to harm." Freda tried to protest, but he silenced her peremptorily. "And the little girl does care for those who belong to her, no matter how she has

131

been treated by them. But now," he continued in a different tone, "I want you to forget all that for the present, though I never can. I want you to think of the day when I first met you, a poor, tired, cold, hungry little girl; and to remember how you gave me your confidence, and chattered to me, and told me I was very kind."

"And so you were," cried Freda eagerly.

"Ah, but I had a motive: I had fallen in love with you."

Freda wriggled her arm out of his, and looked up at him in astonishment. Indeed John Thurley's tone was so robust, matter-of-fact, and dogmatic that this statement was the last she had expected.

"In love with me! Oh!"

And she began to laugh timidly.

"But this is no laughing matter—to me at least," said John Thurley, in a tone more earnest still, and less matter-of-fact. "I tell you I fell in love with you. I suppose you know what that means?"

"Not very well," Freda admitted.

This answer seemed rather to take him aback.

"Why," said he, looking out to sea and frowning with perplexity, "I thought all girls knew that."

"*I* don't," said Freda shaking her head. "I don't understand it at all. It seems ridiculous to like a person very much, fall in love as you call it, when you have only seen that person once, and can't be sure at all what that person is really like."

"Perhaps one can be surer than you think. At any rate I felt sure enough about you to make up my mind at once that you were the girl I should like to make my wife."

"Wife!" echoed Freda in astonishment and even horror, "me! a cripple!"

"Yes, *you*, just as you are, little crutch and all. Now, child, will you have me? You don't love me yet, but you will very soon, for I love you deeply, and you are loving. You trust me, I know, although you have avoided me lately. There is trouble coming upon this part of the world, and I will take you away from it, and keep you safe for all your life. Won't you let me?"

But Freda grew white and began to tremble. Before she could attempt any answer, however, he broke in again.

"I tell you you are not safe here; this place is infested with desperate characters, who have access to the house by all sorts of secret ways. Only this morning, as I was sitting in the library, a man suddenly appeared before me, who seemed to spring out of the wall itself."

In an instant Freda became flushed and full of passionate interest.

"What was he like?" she asked breathlessly.

"He was a young man, with a thin, wolfish face, with light eyes I think; dressed in an old brown shooting jacket. He looked half starved."

The girl's face quivered with distress, and the tears sprang to her eyes and rolled down her cheeks.

"Half starved!" she repeated in a heartbroken voice. "Oh, Dick!"

John Thurley stared at her in attentive silence for a few moments. Then he said drily:

"You are sure you don't know what falling in love is?"

Freda blushed, and began to dry her eyes.

"I know what it is," she answered meekly, "to be sorry for a starving man."

"And you haven't a word for the man who is starving for the love of you?"

There was some passion in his voice now. Freda's breath came quickly; she bent her head in deep thought, and presently raised it to show a face full of excitement, doubt, and entreaty.

"Do you love me enough to do something for my sake? something great, something difficult?"

John Thurley was a practical man, who liked to keep fact and sentiment well apart. A shade of caution came into his tone at once.

"Well, what is it? Let us hear."

"Will you promise"—her voice trembled with passionate eagerness, "not to make any inquiries, not to give any information, about the murder of the man Blewitt?"

She hissed out the last words below her breath.

But John Thurley shook his head at once and decidedly.

"I couldn't allow sentiment to interfere with my duty even for you, my dear," he said in a tone which precluded all hope of his softening. "Besides," he continued decisively, "as a matter-of-fact, I gave all the information I had to the police long since."

Without uttering another word or giving him time for one, Freda fled away as if she had been struck. Running round the angle of the wall, and under one of the clustered arches at the south side of the choir, she stumbled, not seeing where she trod, against a heap of grass-grown masonry, and fell to the ground.

Before she could rise, she heard the voice of the man who had frightened her by jumping up behind the wall of the meadow.

"Beg pardon, Mr. Thurley," said the voice, "but I've come to tell you it's all right. We've followed up the clue you sent, and I've been sent down here to make the arrest. By to-morrow we shall have John Blewitt's murderer safe in quod."

CHAPTER XXIX.

WHEN Freda overheard the words which told her the police were on the track of the murderer, she did not lose a moment in making her way back to the Abbey. Mrs. Bean opened the inner gate, as usual, and was alarmed by the look on the girl's face.

"Why, what's come to you, child?" she said. "Where have you been? Has anybody frightened you again?"

"No," said Freda hoarsely. Then, bending forward, she whispered: "My father—have you seen him?"

"Sh-sh!" said Nell, sharply. "Go into the dining-room."

Freda thought there was a look of anxiety upon the housekeeper's face, but as it was always useless to try to force Nell's confidence, she hurried past her into the dining-room without a word. No one was in the room, however. She was on the point of going back to Mrs. Bean when the corner of a note, which had been thrust under the clock, caught her eye. She pulled it out, and found that it was directed, in her father's handwriting, to "Freda." She opened it eagerly but not without fear. The note was very short:

"MY DEAREST CHILD,—I am away for a little while, you can perhaps guess why. As long as I am out of reach, this Thurley (who is, I believe, an honourable man) can do nothing. You need not be anxious on my account, little one. When I can, I shall come back, and carry you straight back to the convent. I ought never to have brought you away, it is the right place for a little saint. I wish I could have been a better father to you, but it is too late. 'The tree has ta'en the bend.' Good-bye, child.

"Your affectionate,
"FATHER."

Freda sobbed over this; she was surprised to find, among the mingled emotions which the note roused in her, a strong feeling of reluctance to the idea of going back to the convent. The excitement of the strange life she had led since leaving it had spoilt her for the old, calm, passionless existence. What! Never again to leave the shade of those quiet walls? Never to wander, as she now loved to do, about the ruined church of Saint Hilda, whose roofless walls, with their choir of wailing sea-birds, had grown to her ten times more sacred than the little convent-chapel? Never to see her father? Never to see—Dick?

At this thought she broke down, and resting her head upon her hands, let the tears come. And poor Dick had looked half-starved, so John

Thurley said! There began to steal into her heart a consciousness that, *if* things had been different, as it were, and *if* she had not been brought up in, and for, a convent, as one might say, she too might perhaps, to use John Thurley's words, "have known what falling in love was."

She was startled, in the midst of her tears, by the sound of John Thurley's voice in the hall, outside. He was talking to Nell, asking "the way to Oldcastle Farm." Freda sprang up in alarm. What if the farm were her father's hiding-place? It was the probable, the most horrible explanation. The man who had spoken to Thurley that morning was certainly a member of the London police force, and he had said that he was on the murderer's track. It might be, then, that he had got wind of the fact that the farm was to be Captain Mulgrave's hiding-place. If not, what did Mr. Thurley want there?

It took Freda only a few minutes, when these thoughts had occurred to her, to make up her mind what she should do. She waited until, by the more distant sound of their voices, she knew that Thurley and Mrs. Bean had retreated into the passage leading to the precincts of the latter; and then ran upstairs to her own room, dressed hastily for walking, and crept out of the house without being seen by any one.

It was Saturday, and market-day at Presterby. Barnabas Ugthorpe would be at market; and Freda, in her short acquaintance with him, had gained enough insight into that gentleman's tastes and habits to be sure that, instead of making the best of his way home as soon as the business of the day was done, he would at this moment be enjoying himself at the "The Blue Cow," or "The Green Man," or one or other of the small hostelries which abutted on the market-place. So it was in this direction that she turned her steps, flitting among the old grave-stones and hopping down the hundred and ninety-eight worn steps, until she reached Church Street.

It was six o'clock, and the streets swarmed with a noisy rabble. Crowds of children, as usual, played about the steps; riotous fisher-lads, in parties of half-a-dozen or so, streamed into the streets from the Agalyth, a row of tumble-down houses, much out of the perpendicular, that nestled right under the cliff, and some of which fell down, from time to time, into the sea. Knots of women stood gossiping at the doors; girls, in preposterous "best" hats, flaunted down the street in twos and threes. Poor Freda, with her crutch and her quaint dress, was laughed at as she sped along, her progress from time to time impeded by the crowd. At last she reached the little market-place, where business was long since over, but where women were still busy packing up their baskets, and groups of men stood about, discussing the news of the day. At the lower end a line of primitive-looking carts and gigs stretched from one side of the market-place to the other, and straggled into the narrow side-street. From a nest of little beetle-browed and dingy taverns came a noise of mingled merriment, wrangling and loud talking; it was in these unprepossessing quarters she must look for her friend, Freda knew.

The hunt was not a pleasant task. She had to stand some rude "chaff" from the sailor lads, as she stood about the doors peeping in when she could. She was, however, so very simple-minded and unsophisticated, that she bore this ordeal better than an ordinary girl could have done. And then, too, her mind was so steadfastly fixed on its object that many remarks intended for her failed to reach her understanding. She had convinced herself that Barnabas was not in either of the three taverns on the right hand side, and was beginning to despond, when she recognised, among the horseless carts, the one in which the farmer had brought her to the Abbey. Her spirits went up again, and with brisker steps she continued her search. Down into the little side-street she went boldly, and at last with a heart-leap of triumph she ran the farmer to earth.

It was in a narrow slip of an inn that Freda, peeping in at the door, spied the burly Barnabas laying down the law at the bar in a way that he never dared do at home. Indeed, the girl had recognised his voice some yards away. Without the least hesitation, she lifted up her voice, without entering, causing all the guests to look round.

"Barnabas!" was all she said.

The farmer turned as if he had been shot.

"The Lord bless my soul!" he ejaculated. "It's t' little missie!"

"Come," she cried peremptorily, "come at once."

He obeyed as unhesitatingly as if he had received a mandate from the queen. Leaving his glass of ale untasted on the counter, he followed the girl down the street; for without waiting she led the way straight to where his cart stood.

"Get your horse, Barnabas," she said as soon as he came up, "you must drive me to Oldcastle Farm."

"But——" began the bewildered farmer.

She would not let him speak, but stamped her crutch impatiently on the stones. Barnabas was as weak as water with any one who had a will; whistling to himself as if to prove that he was carrying out his own intentions instead of somebody else's, he went straight to the place where his horse was put up. Within ten minutes the cart was jogging down slowly through the crowded street, with Barnabas and Freda side by side on the seat, the farmer shouting to the crowd to keep out of the way.

For a long way they did not exchange a word. As they proceeded down the stone-paved street the throng grew less and less, until, when they got to that point where the houses on the one side give place to the river, they passed only an occasional foot-farer. They were now on the outskirts of Presterby. The lights from the other side twinkled on the water; the distant sounds of the town, and the voices of men calling to each other from the barges, came faintly to their ears. Then for the first time Barnabas, drawing a deep breath, looked down at his companion.

"Eh, but ye're a high-honded lass. What's takin' ye to t' farm?"

"Never mind what's taking me. I have something to say to *you*," said Freda with decision. "Barnabas, you know you didn't keep that secret!"

"What secret?" said he uneasily.

Freda lowered her voice.

"About the dead man, and—the person you found beside him."

Barnabas shuffled his feet.

"Ah doan't knaw as Ah've said a word——"

"Oh, yes, you have. You haven't meant to, perhaps, but you've let out a word here, and a hint there, until——"

Freda stopped. Her voice was breaking.

"Weel, Ah'm downright sorry if Ah have. Mebbe Ah have let aht a word that somebody's picked oop, and—and—weel, Ah hope no harm's coom of it."

"There's only this harm come of it," answered the girl bitterly, "that you have perhaps put the police on the track of—of——"

"A dead mon. Weel, and where's t' harm of that?"

Freda was silent. She had forgotten her father's pretended death.

"Mind ye, missie, there's no good of being too sentimental, and, asking your pardon, t' Capt'n's reputation was none so good, setting aside that little business. So, as Ah said, there's small harm done. And now mebbe you'll tell me what's taking you to Owdcastle Farm. There's ne'er a pleace Ah wouldn't sooner be droiving ye to."

"Why?"

"Because there's bad teales towd of it; an' there's bad characters that goes there."

"Oh, Barnabas, I'm getting used to bad characters. I mean——"

She stopped. The farmer scratched his ear.

"Weel, but it's t' bad characters that are fahnd aht that's t' worst. T' other sort, that keeps dark, aren't near so degreading. An', by what Ah've been told, Ah reckon there's some that's fahnd aht at Owdcastle Farm."

Not a word of explanation of this dark hint could Freda get from him. With Yorkshire obstinacy he shut up his mouth on that one subject, and, although she plied him with entreaties, all that he would add on the subject was:

"Weel, now, ye're warned. Folks that tek' oop wi' dangerous characters must be prepared to tek' t' consequences."

After this speech, Freda fell into frightened silence; and for the rest of the journey there was little conversation between them.

CHAPTER XXX.

FROM time to time, when they got into the open country, Freda was alarmed by the sight of another cart some distance behind them on the road. For long tracts the hedges, the winds in the road, the hills and vales, hid it from her sight, but again and again it would reappear, filling her with misgivings.

"Barnabas," she said at last, when the farmer asked what it was she was turning round to look at so constantly, "there's another cart following us; I am sure of it. Who do you think it is?"

"Fred Barlow, moast loike," answered he, with a glance back. "He's generally home early, an' he lives only two moile aweay from wheer Ah do."

And there was silence again.

But Freda was not satisfied; however long it might be before it reappeared, that cart was sure to come in sight again, and as for Fred Barlow, he would surely come in a little vehicle the size of the one she was driving in, not in a big, lumbering conveyance like that! Before Barnabas turned up the lane that led to the farm, though, the big cart had been lost sight of for so long that the girl's fears had calmed a little, and by the time they drew up at the front door, she had forgotten everything but Dick, and the object of her journey.

Barnabas got down and pulled the bell, but no one answered. He pulled it a second time, and came back to speak to Freda.

"Toimes are changed here," he said, with a sagacious nod. "Ye woan't find a merry welcome and troops of servants to weait on ye this toime."

As nobody had yet come to the door, he gave it a kick with his hob-nailed boots, and called out lustily:

"Here, here! Is noabody cooming to open this door? Here's a leady weating, an' aht of respect to t' sex, Ah'll burst t' door in if soombody doan't open it!"

This frank-spoken summons succeeded. The door opened at once and Dick looked out. But was it Dick, this haggard, cavernous-eyed creature with his clothes hanging loosely upon him? He looked like a hunted criminal, and Freda felt a great shock as she noted the change.

"What do you want?" asked he shortly.

"Ask t' leady," said Barnabas in the same tone.

Dick started when he caught sight of the girl.

"*You!* Miss Mulgrave!"

She held out her hands.

"Help me down, please," she said in a husky voice, "I want to speak to you. Let me come inside."

"Are you coming too?" said Dick, not very graciously, to Ugthorpe, as he helped Freda down.

"No, no, don't you come, Barnabas," said the girl quickly, turning to the farmer. "I want to speak to Dick by himself. You wait for me."

Barnabas, laughed with some constraint.

"Ah doan't knaw what Ah'm to seay to that."

"Why, do as she wishes. She shan't come to any harm, Ugthorpe," said Dick with a break in his voice.

But the farmer still hesitated.

"Ah'm not afreaid of you, Mr. Richard. But—who have ye gotten abaht t' pleace?"

Dick flushed as he answered quickly: "Nobody who can or will do any harm to Miss Mulgrave."

This answer, while it reassured Barnabas, alarmed Freda. For it seemed to confirm her fears that it was her father who was in hiding about the farm.

"Yes, Barnabas, let me go," she urged, touching his arm in entreaty.

"Well, Ah give ye ten minutes, an' ye must leave t' door open, and when toime 's oop, Ah shall fetch ye."

"Thank you, thank you, good, dear Barnabas," said she.

But he began instantly to scoff.

"Oh, yes, we're angels while we let ye have your own weay, an' devils if we cross ye. Ye're not t' first woman Ah've hed to deal with, missie," he grumbled.

But Freda did not heed him. She was walking very demurely down the unlighted passage with Dick, saying never a word now she had got her own way, and keeping close to the wall as if afraid of her companion. He felt bound to try to make conversation.

"I'm afraid you'll find a great change in the place since my aunt left, Miss Mulgrave. This is only a bachelor's den now, and you know a man with no ladies to look after him is not famous for his orderliness, and in fact—I'm hardly settled here yet you know."

They were passing through the passage, at right angles with the entrance-hall, which ran alongside the servants' quarters. No sounds of merry talk and laughter now, no glimpses of a roaring fire through the half-open kitchen door. Nothing but cold and damp, and a smell as of rooms long shut-up to which the fresh air never came. Freda shivered, but it was not with cold; it was with horror of the gloom and loneliness of the place. Poor Dick! They passed into the huge ante-room; it was entirely unlighted, and Dick turned to offer her his hand.

"You will hurt yourself, against the—walls. There is nothing else for you to hurt yourself against," he added rather bitterly.

She gave him her hand; it was trembling.

"You are not frightened, are you? If you knew what it is to me to touch a kind hand again, and—and yours——"

He stopped short, putting such a strong constraint upon himself that Freda felt he was trembling from head to foot.

"Don't, don't," she whispered.

Dick made haste to laugh, as if at a joke. But it was a poor attempt at merriment and woke hoarse echoes in the old rafters. They had reached the door of the banqueting-hall.

"You must be prepared for an awfully great change here," he said, with assumed cheerfulness. "My aunt wanted the furniture of this room; of course she didn't think I should use such a big place all by myself. But I've got used to it, so I stick to it in its bareness. You won't mind my showing you in here; the fact is the—the—drawing-room's locked up."

"No-o," quavered Freda, who knew that all the furniture of the farm had been seized and sold either before or immediately after Mrs. Heritage's departure, "not at all. In fact I would rather."

"I don't know about that," rejoined Dick dubiously as he opened the door.

All this had not prepared the girl for the desolate sight which met her eyes. The great hall, which had looked so handsome with its rugs, its old oak furniture and tapestry hangings, was barer than a prison ward. A vast expanse of floor, once brightly polished, now scratched and dirty; rough, bare walls with nothing to hide their nakedness, formed a picture so dreary that she uttered a low cry. In the huge fireplace a small wood fire burned low; an old retriever, crippled with age and rheumatism, wagged his tail feebly without rising at his master's approach, and gave a feeble growl for the stranger. A kitchen chair, with some of the rails missing; a small deal table; an arrangement of boxes against the wall covered by a man's ulster; these formed all the furniture of the huge room. Freda stopped short when she had advanced a few steps; and burst into tears. Dick affected to laugh boisterously.

"I didn't reckon on the effect these rough diggings would have on a lady," he said, in a tone of forced liveliness which did not deceive his guest. "Why, this is a palace to some of the places I've stayed in when in the Highlands. A man doesn't want many luxuries when he's alone. But I suppose it shocks you."

"Ye-es, it does," sobbed Freda.

"Come and take a chair. I'm sorry there isn't much choice; I've ordered a couple of those wicker ones with cushions, but they haven't come yet. I'll sit upon the sofa."

But Freda knew that the pile of boxes on which he seated himself, carelessly nursing his knee, was his bed. She had regained command of herself, however, so she took his only chair, and looked steadily into the fire. Dick sprang up again immediately, and affected to look about him with much eagerness.

"What an idiot I am!" he exclaimed. "I believe I've forgotten to bring in any candles; I know I was out of them last night."

Freda said nothing, but sat very still. The tears were silently rolling down her cheeks again. She waited while he rummaged in the table drawer, and opened the door by the fireplace, as if in search. Then quick as lightning, while his back was turned, she whipped out from under her long cloak a large neat brown paper parcel, unrolled it, and took out two candles, which she proceeded to fix on the table by the primitive schoolgirl fashion of melting the ends at the fire. Then she took out of the parcel a box of matches, and lit the candles. In the meantime Dick had returned from his fruitless errand, and was watching her helplessly from the other side of the table. When she had finished, Freda dared not look at him, but tried furtively to draw towards her the tell-tale parcel, out of which several small packages had rolled. But at last she made a bold dash, and with a shaking voice said:

"I know better than you think what a man is, left to himself. I know—you've forgotten—to get in—any supper."

By the time she reached the last words, her voice had dropped to a guttural whisper. But she was so much excited that it was quite easy for her to laugh long and naturally, as she opened, one after another, a series of little packages, and spread them out before his eyes.

"There's butter and bacon, and a piece of cold beef, and tea, and sugar, and even bread!" she ended in a shrill scream, with her breath coming and going in quick sobs.

For, glancing up, she had caught on Dick's face, which looked more haggard than ever in the candle light, the terrible look of hunger, real, famishing hunger. She looked down again quickly at her provisions.

"Aha!" she cried in a quavering voice, "*I* know how to take care of myself! *I* wasn't going to trust myself to the tender mercies of a man!"

Dick said nothing, but she talked on with scarcely a pause.

"You've got some plates, I suppose, and one knife and fork at least. Go and fetch them. Make haste, make haste!"

And she rattled her crutch upon the floor. The old dog was hungry too; he came sniffing and barking about her, as if he knew that she had brought help to him and his master. Dick had some plates and knives and forks, and a broken teapot. These Freda arranged upon the table with nimble, graceful fingers. For the moment, moved by the unguessed extremities to which her host was reduced, she had forgotten that the chief object of her visit was one of warning.

She was recalled to the truth in a startling manner. A handful of earth and stones was flung up at one of the lofty windows by some one in the court-yard. Freda sprang forward with a cry, her worst fears confirmed; as Dick turned hastily from the table, she clung to his arm and tried to speak. But at first words refused to come.

CHAPTER XXXI.

WHEN Freda recovered her voice, Dick had broken away from her restraining touch, and was moving, in a hesitating sort of way, towards the door.

"Dick?" cried the girl in a frightened whisper, "Listen! I had forgotten why I came. There are men coming here, perhaps to-night, policemen from London, I think. Is—he—safe?"

Dick started, and began to tremble violently.

"Great Heavens!" he said in a hoarse voice, "how did *you* know? How did *you* hear? Is it known all over the place?"

"I don't know," said Freda sadly, "but I don't think it is. Barnabas didn't seem to know anything about it."

He stood still for a moment, considering.

"Men coming here, you say! You are sure of that?"

"I am not sure that they are coming to-night, but they will come sooner or later. One said they knew where he was, and the other asked the way to Oldcastle Farm."

Dick turned to her quickly and decisively.

"Do you mind if I leave you here alone for a little while?"

"No-o, but won't you let me come too? Oh, do let me!"

"I can't. It would only alarm him the more. You stay here, and if you hear any one at the front door, don't take any notice, but come across the yard as softly as you can; and if you see a light shining through a grating close to the ground on the other side, throw a stone through, but don't cry out."

"Very well," said Freda.

As Dick turned again to go, the provisions laid out on the table caught his eye. With a hotly flushing face, he took up the bread and cutting off a piece, said, with an awkward laugh:

"We may as well give him some supper, don't you think so?"

Without a word, Freda loaded him with meat, bread and butter.

"The tea isn't ready yet," she whispered. "I'll make it, and you can come back for that."

He nodded and went off, not without trying to utter some husky thanks, which the girl would not hear. He had one of her candles and a box of matches in his pocket. Left alone in the great bare room, poor Freda felt all the womanish fears which the need of active exertion had kept off for so long. Terror on her father's account, grief for poor starving Dick; above all, an awestruck fear that God would not forgive such black crimes as some of those laid to their account, caused the bitter tears to roll down her cheeks, while her lips moved in simple-hearted prayer for them.

Presently the old dog, whom she had been feeding, pricked up his ears and growled ominously. She sprang to her feet, but at first heard nothing. Crossing the floor quickly and lightly, she opened the door and listened. Somebody at the front of the house was knocking. The summons, however, was neither loud nor imperative, and she crept through the passages, fancying that it might perhaps be only Barnabas Ugthorpe who had come back for her. Creeping into the deserted kitchen, she peeped through the dusty panes of the window, which was heavily barred. She could just see the outline of a large hooded cart, and a couple of men standing beside it. At once she knew it was the cart which had followed Barnabas Ugthorpe's.

Retreating from the window as noiselessly as she had come while the intermittent knocking at the front door went on a little louder than before, she returned through the passage and slipped into the court-yard. She knew where to look for the grating of which Dick had spoken, having noticed it in the course of her investigations on the occasion of her previous visit. It consisted of two iron bars placed perpendicularly across a small opening in the wall of the very oldest part of the building—the portion known as "the dungeons." Freda crept to the grating and stooped down. Yes, there was a light inside. She took up a handful of earth and stones, as she had been told to do, and threw them in with a trembling hand.

Instantly the light was extinguished.

Freda stole away from the grating, afraid that if the front door were burst open and the police were to find her there, her presence might afford a clue to her father's hiding-place. If she got on to the top of the old outer wall, she thought, she might watch the course of events without herself being seen. She had hardly reached this post of vantage when she heard a crash and a noise as of splintering wood, and a few moments later she saw the black figures of half a dozen men dispersed about the court-yard below. She was crouching down in the narrow path that ran along the ruinous old wall, and peeping over the fringe of dried grass and brambles which grew along the edge. Suddenly she felt a hand placed roughly over her mouth and eyes, so that she could neither see nor cry out. After the first moment, she did not attempt to do either, but remained quite still, not knowing in whose grasp she was. She heard the man breathing hard, felt that his hands trembled, and knew that he was in a paroxysm of physical terror. Was it her father himself? That thought would have kept her quiet, even if his rough clasp had been rougher still. As it was, the pressure of his hand caused her teeth to cut through her under-lip.

Crouching still in the same cramped attitude, and still gagged and blindfolded by the mysterious hand, she presently heard a stealthy footfall close behind, and then a whispered word or two.

"Let her go," hissed Dick's voice peremptorily.

The next moment Freda felt herself free, heard a soft thud on the earth below, and saw the figure of a man crouching close under the wall on the outer side.

"Oh, Dick, will he get safe away?" she whispered, breathing the word close to his ear.

"I don't know," answered Dick gloomily. "Sh! Keep quiet."

But they had already been seen. In a very short time the men in the yard below had found their way up, and Freda and her companion found themselves flanked on either side by a stalwart policeman.

"Hallo!" cried a voice from the court-yard, which Freda recognised as Thurley's, "have you got him?"

Dick said nothing, but Freda, moved by a sudden, overpowering impulse, threw her arms round his neck and cried aloud:

"No, no!"

Thurley spoke again, in a hard, altered voice.

"Bring them both down here," he said sharply.

But Dick would not suffer a strange man's hand to touch the girl.

"I will take her down," he said quietly.

And, escorted by a policeman in front and another behind, they made their way down into the court-yard, and were conducted to John Thurley, who, with a police-officer in plain clothes, evidently took the lead in this expedition.

"What are you doing with that young lady?" asked Thurley harshly.

"That is no business of yours," answered Dick. "By what authority have you forced your way into my house?"

Thurley was about to answer, but the police-officer with him spoke instead, in a conciliatory tone.

"You see, sir, we've got a search-warrant."

And he produced a document at which Dick glanced hastily.

"Very well," he said shortly. "But you won't find any one here!"

"I hope not, sir," said the man, touching his hat and stepping back.

Meanwhile Thurley, a good deal agitated by the discovery of Freda's presence, was trying to persuade her to let him send her back to the Abbey at once. She refused simply but firmly; and turning her back upon him, went straight to Dick, who had withdrawn a little from the group. Thurley went up to him.

"If you have any of the feelings of a man," he said, "which perhaps is not likely, you will persuade this young lady to go back to her friends."

"I am with one of them now," cried Freda, clinging to Dick's arm.

"I think," said Dick, whose deep voice was trembling, "that you had better go back to your manhunting, and not insult people who have done you no harm."

"I have a right to interfere on behalf of this lady. I love her."

"So do I," said Dick in a low voice.

"*You!*"

"And Dick has more right to say so than you," broke in Freda's clear voice, shaking with feeling, "for I love him!"

Dick pressed her arm against his side, but he did not speak. Neither did John Thurley, but he reeled back a step, as if he had received a blow. Then, with a shrug of the shoulders which was meant to be contemptuous, but which was only crestfallen and disgusted, he turned away and left the young fellow with Freda, while he rejoined the search-party.

Neither Dick nor his companion spoke for some minutes. In all the misery of this strange situation, with the messengers of the law hunting high and low around them for a man who had incurred the penalty of death, the new and strange delight each felt of touching a loving hand, deadened the anxiety and the pain. Each felt the intoxication of the knowledge that each was loved. Dick spoke first; he looked down into the girl's face and said gently:

"I am afraid you are cold, dear."

She shook her head.

"No, no, no," she whispered, "if they hear you say that, they will take me away."

He led her back into the house, and wished to place her in the one chair by the fireplace in the banqueting-hall. But she would not take it.

"Eat," she whispered. "If they find you having your supper quietly they will be more likely to believe that there is no one here."

This was undeniably a good suggestion; and Dick took advantage of it. But hungry as he was, having indeed been half-starved of late, he would have eaten little but for Freda's insistence. She waited on him herself, cutting bread and butter, making the tea, hovering about like a good spirit. He, however, having hungered for more than bread during these solitary latter days, would have neglected the food before him to watch her tender eyes, to kiss her little hands. But whenever he turned from the table, he felt a peremptory touch on his shoulder, and heard a stamp of Freda's crutch and her commanding voice saying:

"Eat, eat!"

So the minutes passed by, and their spirits began to rise. For, although they did not tell each other so in so many words, both felt that on this great happiness which was stealing upon them the shadow of a great misfortune could not come.

When he had finished his supper, Dick drew his one chair to the fireside, made Freda sit in it, and curled himself up on the ground at her feet.

"Isn't it strange," said the girl, "that they leave us alone so long? You don't think they have gone away, do you?"

"No such luck, I'm afraid."

"Hadn't we better go out and see what they are doing?"

"Why should we leave off being happy any sooner then we need?"

"What do you mean, Dick? You don't think they've—caught him?" whispered she in alarm.

"No, and I don't think they will catch him. But when we leave this room we shall be just strangers for the rest of our lives."

"But we shan't! Oh, Dick, do you think I would ever treat you as a stranger?"

"You won't be able to help yourself," said he, looking up at her with a dreary smile. "You are so ridiculously ignorant of the world, little one, and you've been so neglected since you've been here that I don't know how to explain the smallest thing to you without frightening you. But I assure you that after this escapade to-night you will never be allowed to go out by yourself again."

"Escapade!"

"Yes. That is what you will hear your expedition called, and you will never be allowed to make another. Quite right too. If you had been left to run wild here, you would have been spoilt, and you would have begun to mix up right with wrong like the rest of us."

"I don't think so," said Freda gently. "I should have been told the difference."

"But who was there to tell you?"

"God would have told me."

There was a pause, and then Dick said:

"You're a Roman Catholic, aren't you?"

"No, I was not allowed to be one."

"Well, what are you then?"

Freda looked puzzled, and rather grieved.

"I don't know, I'm sure."

"If you're religious, you must belong to some religion, you know."

"Well, I'm a Christian. Isn't that enough religion?"

"I've never met any sort of Christian who would admit that it was."

Freda sighed.

"I am afraid mine is a religion all to myself then. But somehow," and she lowered her voice reverently, "I don't believe it makes any difference to God."

"I don't suppose it does," said Dick gently. "I think," he went on presently, "judging by its effect on you, I would rather have your religion than any other."

"I wish you would, then," she rejoined eagerly. "For then you could never do wrong things and think they were right."

"How shall I begin?"

"Go to church."

"What church?"

"It doesn't matter. Sister Agnes used to say that in every church in the world there was some good spoken to those who wanted to hear it."

"I wonder what good Sister Agnes would have heard from old Staynes?"

"Something, you may be sure. Or, how would his wife be such a noble woman?"

More pleased by her ingenuousness than convinced by her arguments, Dick promised that he would go to church, to the delight of Freda, who thought she had secured a great moral victory.

They had forgotten the police, who were searching the house; they had forgotten the jealous Thurley; when again the old dog, half opening his eyes, gave a low growl of warning. Dick jumped up and faced the door. There was no enemy, but Barnabas Ugthorpe, wearing a very grave and troubled face.

"What is it? Speak out, man," cried Dick impatiently.

"Let me teake t' little leady aweay first, mester."

Dick staggered.

"They haven't—caught him, Barnabas?"

"Ah'm afreaid so."

Low as he spoke, Freda caught the words. Overcome with self-reproach for having momentarily forgotten her father's danger, with misery at his unhappy plight, she tottered across the room towards the farmer, who, lifting her up in his arms as if she had been a child, carried her straight out of the room, to the front door of the farm-house.

CHAPTER XXXII.

THE covered cart, in which the police had come, had now disappeared. Beside Barnabas Ugthorpe's cart was a gig, with John Thurley standing at the horse's head.

"This way," said Thurley in a peremptory tone, as Barnabas was carrying the girl to his own cart, "I'm going back to the Abbey and can take Miss Mulgrave with me."

Freda shuddered. The farmer said a soothing word in her ear, and without heeding Mr. Thurley's directions, placed her on the seat on which she had come.

"If it's t' seame to you, sir, Ah'll tak' t' leady mysen."

"Pray, are you the young lady's guardian?"

"Ah've as mooch reght to t' neame as you, sir," answered Barnabas surlily. And without waiting for further parley, the farmer got up in his seat and drove away.

Freda and her driver made their way back to the Abbey almost in silence. All that he would tell her about the capture of the murderer was that "t' poor fellow was caught in a field at back o' t' house."

Mrs. Bean was waiting at the lodge-gates for her, and Freda saw by the housekeeper's white face that she had heard the result of the expedition.

"Oh, Mrs. Bean, it is too horrible; I can't bear it!" sobbed the girl, throwing her arms round Nell's neck.

But the housekeeper pushed her off with a "Sh!" and a frightened look round, and Freda saw that John Thurley was standing in the deep shadow under the gateway. With a sudden cry the girl stepped back, and would have run away to Barnabas, whose cart was just moving off, if Thurley had not started forward, led her within the gates with a strong but gentle hand, and closed them behind her. He would not let her go until they had reached the dining-room; then he apologised rather brusquely, and asked her to sit down.

"I can hear what you have to say standing," she said in a low, breathless voice.

"Why are you so changed to me? Why did you run away from me just now?" asked Thurley, distressed and irritated. "It is by your invitation I am here; you have only to say you are tired of my presence, and late as it is I will go out and try to find some other lodging."

The instincts of a gentlewoman were too strong in Freda for her not to be shocked at the idea of showing incivility to a guest, however ill he might have requited her hospitality. She overcame the abhorrence she felt at his conduct sufficiently to say:

"You are very welcome to stay here as long as you please, Mr. Thurley. If my conduct towards you has changed, I hope you will own that it was not without reason."

"But I think it is," said he stoutly. "It's all to your interest that this nest of smugglers should be cleared out; and as for a certain cowardly criminal whom we have had to take up for something worse, why, *you* have no reason, beyond your natural kindness of heart, to be sorry he has met his deserts."

Without answering him, and with much dignity, Freda turned to leave the room. But the words he hastened to add arrested her attention.

"To-morrow I have to return to London. Now as there may be scenes in this place not fit for a lady to witness, in the course of breaking up this gang, I intend to take you away with me, and to put you under proper care."

"Will you send me back to the convent?" asked Freda eagerly.

John Thurley, who had a strong dislike to "popery" frowned.

"No," he said decidedly, "I can't do that. But I will undertake to have you well cared for."

Freda paused one moment at the door, looking very thoughtful.

"Thank you," she then said simply, as, with her eyes on the floor, she turned the handle; "good-night!"

There was something in her manner which made John Thurley, inexperienced as he was in women's ways, suspect that she meant to trick him. Therefore, from the moment she left her room on the following morning, she felt that she was watched. Mrs. Bean had evidently gone over to the enemy, being indeed convinced that John Thurley's plan was a good and kind one. When Freda announced her intention of going to church, the housekeeper said she would go with her. Freda made no objection, though as Mrs. Bean never went to church, her intention was evident. Old Mrs. Staynes was delighted to see the girl, and thanked her for coming.

"Why," said Freda in surprise, "I should have come long ago, only I didn't know you, and I was afraid."

"Two blessings in one day!" whispered the little woman ingenuously.

And she glanced towards one of the free pews, where Freda, with a throb of delight, saw Dick's curly head bending over his hat.

Only once, throughout the entire service, did Freda dare to meet his eyes, although they were, as she knew, fixed upon her all the time. When she did so, she was so much shocked that the tears rushed into her eyes. Pale, haggard, deathly, he scarcely looked like a living man; while the great yearning that burned in his blue eyes seemed to pierce straight to her own heart. She had to bite her lips to keep back the cry that rose to them: "Dick, Dick!"

When the service was over, he disappeared before the rest of the congregation had moved from their seats. Poor Freda tottered as she went out, and had to lean for support on Mrs. Bean. She had forgotten that the story of her father's crime and capture would be likely to be in every one's mouth that morning; the whispering groups gathering in the churchyard suddenly woke her to this fact, and stung her to put forth all her strength to reach the Abbey quickly. John Thurley met her at the gates.

"You will have to make haste with your packing," he said abruptly but not unkindly, "our train goes at four."

"I will see to that," said Nell.

Freda said nothing at all. She passed the other two, and went into the house, and appeared, in due time, quiet and composed, at the dinner-table.

When the meal was over, Thurley told her to go and put on her things. She rose obediently and left the room; but instead of going to her own apartment, she went to the library, and finding the secret door as she had left it, closed, but not locked, had little difficulty in opening it, and in securing it behind her. Now Thurley knew of this door, since he had seen Dick come through it; so to secure herself from pursuit in case he should guess where she had gone, Freda closed the trap-door at the head of the narrow staircase, and bolted it securely. Then, running down the second staircase, she locked herself into the room where her father had made himself known to her, and as a last precautionary measure, let herself down the rope ladder into the cellar beneath.

He must go to London without her now!

The triumphant thought had scarcely flashed through her mind when, with a start, she became aware that she was not alone. A man was creeping stealthily from the opposite side of the room towards her.

CHAPTER XXXIII.

FREDA was by this time getting too much accustomed to the shifts and surprises of the smugglers' haunt to be greatly alarmed by the discovery that she was not alone in the underground chamber. Besides, her indignation against Thurley gave her a fellow-feeling with even the most lawless of the men he had been sent to spy upon. So she cried out in a clear voice:

"It is I, Freda Mulgrave; I have come down here to escape being carried off to London by John Thurley. Who are you?"

The man raised to the level of his face a dark lantern, turning its rays full upon himself. The girl, in spite of the fact that she was prepared to keep her feelings well under control, gave a cry of joy.

It was her father.

Freda stretched out her arms to him, trembling, frightened, crying with misery and with joy.

"You have escaped!" she whispered. "Escaped! Oh, what can I do to help you? to save you?"

Captain Mulgrave laughed, but with a quiver in his voice, as he smoothed her bright hair.

"Calm down, child," he said kindly. "I—I want to talk to you. Come with me to the ruins! I want to get out to the daylight, where I can see your little face."

"But, father, John Thurley may still be about. He wanted to take me away to London this afternoon, and I came down here to be safe. Perhaps——"

"Never mind him. He shan't take you anywhere unless you want to go. Come with me."

Surprised by the tone he took, which was not that of a hunted man, Freda followed her father in silence along the underground passage, and up the steps into the ruined church. Captain Mulgrave then helped his daughter up the broken steps which led to the window in the west front, and they sat down on the old stones and looked out to the sea. A conviction which had been growing in Freda's mind as they came along, brightening her eyes and making her heart beat wildly, became stronger than ever when he deliberately chose this spot, in full view of any one who might stroll through the ruins. It was a grey, cold day, with a drizzle of rain falling; the sea was all shades of murky green and brown, with little crests of foam appearing and disappearing; the sea-birds flew in and out restlessly about the worn grey arches, screaming and flapping their wide wings; the wind blew keen and straight from the northwest, but Freda did not know that she was bitterly cold, and that her lips and fingers were blue, for her heart and her head were on fire.

"Father," she whispered, crouching near him and looking into his face, "forgive me for what I thought. Oh, I see it was not true, and I could die of joy!"

She was shaking from head to foot, panting with excitement. Captain Mulgrave looked affectionately into her glowing face.

"Why, child," he said, "there wasn't a man or woman in England who wouldn't have condemned me! Why should you blame yourself. When Barnabas Ugthorpe caught me, as he thought, red-handed, I saw that nothing but a miracle could save my neck; if I lived, it was sure to leak out. So I died. And they buried the murdered man instead of me."

"But father, the jury—were they all in the secret!"

"No. They viewed a live body instead of a dead one. I had a beautifully painted wound on my breast, and I lay in the coffin till I was as cold as the dead; and I took care that the jury shouldn't be warm enough to want to hang about long, or to have much sensitiveness of touch left if they were inclined to be curious."

"But, father, wouldn't it have been less risk just to go away?"

"No, for my disappearance would have told against me at the inevitable time, when Barnabas should babble out his secret. I thought, too, that my supposed death would put the real murderer off his guard, and that I might be able to track him down in the end."

"Did you know who it was?" she asked in a whisper, after a pause.

"I guessed—and guessed correctly."

"Who was it?"

"Bob Heritage."

"And they have caught him?"

"Last night, hiding about the old farm-house. I went away yesterday in my yacht, because I had got wind of the search, and thought they were after *me*. This morning I came sneaking back to find out whether you were safe, and Crispin was on the scaur with the news."

Freda listened to these details, conscious, though she would not have owned it, of a secret disappointment in the midst of her joy at learning her father's innocence. In spite of the kindness he showed when he was with her, she was to him only an afterthought. He had made no provision for her safety yesterday, left her no directions for her protection in the time of trouble which was coming. One other consideration grieved her deeply: the shame and distress which had been lifted from her shoulders now fell upon those of poor Dick. These thoughts caused her to drop into a silence which her father made no attempt to break. While they were still sitting side by side without exchanging a word, they heard the click of the gate behind, and a man's voice saying "Thank you" to the lodge-keeper. It was John Thurley.

Captain Mulgrave and he caught sight of each other at the same moment, and the former at once came down. The meeting between the two men was a strange one. Each held out his hand, but with diffidence. Thurley spoke first.

"Captain Mulgrave," said he, "I am indeed sorry that I should have been the means of bringing justice down upon you. At the same time I must say I should have thought that a man who had served his country so well would be the last to have any hand in defrauding her."

Captain Mulgrave laughed harshly.

"'My country' rated my services so highly that in return for them they turned me off like a dog. 'My country' made me an outlaw by her treatment; let 'my country' take the blame of my reprisals."

"I should have expected more magnanimity from you."

"To every man his own virtues; none of the meeker ones are among mine," said the other grimly. "I have been disgraced and left to eat my heart out for fifteen years. And I tell you I think the debt between my country and me is still all on her side."

"Perhaps your country begins to think so too. At any rate the government, I feel sure, would be reluctant to prosecute you, as it would have done anybody else in your case. For it would not be only smuggling against you, Captain Mulgrave; it would be conspiracy."

"The government knows, as well as I do, that prosecution of me would lead to unpleasant inquiries and reminiscences. The same party is in now that was in at the time of my disgrace; and as we are on the eve of a general election, my case would make a very good handle for the opposite side to use."

"Well, don't count on that too much. You can't deny it is a serious offence to form such an organisation for illegal purposes as you have done. This place must be cleared out, the underground passages (which I know all about) blocked up; and if you don't find it convenient to leave England for a time, I am afraid you'll find that your past services won't save you from arrest."

"The organisation is better worked than you think; my going away will not break it up. There's another good head in it."

"If you mean Crispin Bean's, it is a good head indeed. On finding, this morning, that the game was up, he came to me and gave me full details of the band, its working, names, everything."

Captain Mulgrave was not only astonished, he was incredulous.

"The d——l he did!" he muttered.

And it was not until John Thurley had read him out some notes he had taken down during Crispin's confession, that the master of Sea-Mew Abbey would believe that his lieutenant had gone over to the enemy. Then he shrugged his shoulders and chose a cigar very carefully.

"Will you have one?" he said, offering the case to Thurley. "They smoke none the worse for being contraband."

John Thurley declined.

"Ah, well," continued the other, "I bear you no ill-will for causing my expatriation, especially as in doing so you have cleared my name of a charge I saw no means of disproving. By-the-bye, why didn't you speak out sooner about the murder?"

"Because I had no very strong evidence myself. I put the case in the hands of the police, and detectives were sent down here who discovered that a man on horseback had come from Oldcastle Farm on the day of the murder, that he had tied up his horse in a shed at the bottom of the hill, just outside the town, and had been seen with a revolver in his hand making his way across the field to the spot where Barnabas Ugthorpe found the body. The man was identified as Robert Heritage; it was found out that he had just learnt the servant's intention to betray his master's secrets to you. This is evidence enough to try the man on, if not to hang him."

"And the cousin, what becomes of him?"

This was the question Freda had been dying to ask, and she drew near, clasping her hands tightly in her anxiety to learn Dick's fate.

"I don't quite know. He seems to have been used as a tool from a very early age by his good-for-nothing cousin. It's an exceedingly awkward business, especially for me, as I am distantly connected with the family, and I feel for the poor lady very much. I must look into their affairs, and try to get the farm let for her benefit. As for this Dick, he had better emigrate."

"He won't do that," interrupted Freda quickly.

"He would rather starve than leave his old home!"

Both gentlemen turned in surprise, for the girl spoke with feeling and fire. John Thurley looked hurt and angry, her father only amused.

"What do you know about the young rascal's sentiments?" asked the latter.

"I only know what he told me," she answered simply, with a blush.

There was a pause in the talk for a few minutes. Then Captain Mulgrave said:

"We might go over to the farm this afternoon, and see the fellow."

The other assented without alacrity. There was another person to be provided for, whose welfare interested him more than that of a hundred young men.

"What about your daughter?" he asked in a constrained voice.

"Oh, Freda's going back to the convent. You have always wanted to, haven't you, child?"

"Yes, father," answered the girl, who had, however, suddenly fallen a-trembling at the suggestion.

"I—I could have provided for her better than that, if—if she had chosen," said John Thurley, blushing as shyly as a girl, and finding a difficulty in getting his words out.

"Eh! *You?* cried Captain Mulgrave. Do you mean that you thought of marrying my little lame girl? Here, Freda, what do you say to that?"

Freda blushed and kept her eyes on the ground.

"I say, father, that I am very much obliged to Mr. Thurley, but I would rather go back to the convent, if you please."

"You hear that, Mr. Thurley? I told you so. The child was born for a nun—takes to the veil as a duck does to water."

But John Thurley did not feel so sure of that, and he looked troubled.

When, later in the day, the dogcart stood at the door waiting for the two gentlemen, they found Freda standing beside it in her outdoor dress.

"What, little one, are you going with us?" asked Captain Mulgrave.

"Yes, if you will please take me, father."

"Well, as you're going to see so little more of the world, I suppose you must be humoured. Jump up in front. Mr. Thurley, will you drive, or shall I?"

"You drive one way, and I the other, if you will let me."

"All right. You'll take the reins coming back then."

And Freda saw by the expression of John Thurley's face that he was too much annoyed to wish to sit by her just then.

CHAPTER XXXIV.

It was getting dark when the dogcart drove up to Oldcastle Farm. The front door which had been partly destroyed by the forcible entry of the police was open, and both gentlemen were inclined to the conclusion that the lonely tenant of the house had left it. They were confirmed in this opinion when, on ringing the bell, they found no notice taken of their summons.

"Poor lad's turned it up," said Captain Mulgrave turning to Thurley with a nod.

"It looks like it."

They tied the horse up to an iron ring in the farm-house wall provided for such purposes, and went inside, leaving Freda, who now hung back a little, to come in or not, as she pleased. As soon as the two gentlemen had gone down the entrance hall, Freda slipped in after them, and waited to see which way they would turn. After a glance into the rooms to right and left, they went through into the court-yard. Taking for granted that Dick had at last followed the only possible course of abandoning the old shell of what had been his boyhood's home, they were going, by Thurley's demand, to explore those recesses where the smuggled goods had formerly been stored.

Freda knew better than they. Tripping quickly through the empty rooms and passages, she reached the door of the banqueting-hall, but was suddenly seized with a fit of shyness when she heard the sound of a man coughing. However, she conquered this feeling sufficiently to open the door under cover of the noise Dick made in poking the fire, and then she stood just inside, shy again. Dick felt the draught from the open door, turned and saw her. He was sitting in his own chair by the fire, with the old dog still at his feet. The shadows were already black under the high windows on the side of the court-yard, but the light from the west was still strong enough for Freda to see a flash of pleasure come into his face as he caught sight of her.

"You have a bad cold," she said in a constrained voice, coming shyly forward as he almost ran to meet her.

"Yes, there's a broken window up there," said he, glancing upwards, "and—and the curtains the spiders make are not very thick."

"Poor Dick!"

She said it in such a heartfelt tone of commiseration that the tears came into his eyes, and when she saw them, a sympathetic mist came over her eyes too.

"They think you have gone away," she said in a whisper, glancing up at the windows which overlooked the court-yard, "but I knew better!"

"Who are 'they'?"

"My father and Mr. Thurley."

"Your father! I didn't know that he was alive till yesterday. What will he do? There will be all sorts of difficulties about the trick he played."

"He will have to go away. But he seems rather glad; he is tired of living up here, he says."

She spoke rather sadly.

"And you?" said Dick.

"Oh, I'm not tired of it. I think the old Abbey-church the most beautiful place in the world. I should like to spend my life here."

"And will you go away with him?"

"No, he is going to take me back to the convent."

"What! For ever? For altogether? Will you be a nun?"

"Yes."

"Do you like that?" asked Dick very earnestly, "to go and waste your youth and your prettiness, shut up with a lot of sour old women who were too ugly to get themselves husbands?"

Freda laughed a little.

"Oh, you don't know anything about it," she said, shaking her head, "they are not at all like that."

"But do you seriously like the thought of going back as much as you liked the thought of being a nun before you left the convent?"

There was a long pause. At last:

"No-o," said Freda very softly. "But—it's better than what I should have had to do if I hadn't chosen that!"

"What was that?"

"Marry Mr. Thurley."

Dick started and grew very red.

"Oh, yes, it is better than that, much better," he assented heartily.

"Yes, I—I thought you'd think so."

She said this because they were both getting rather flurried and excited, and she felt a little awkward. Both were leaning against the table, and tapping their fingers on it. Something therefore had to be said, but in a moment she felt it was not the right thing. For Dick began to breathe hard, and to grow restless, as he said quickly:

"You see it's not as if some young fellow of a suitable age, whom you—whom you—rather liked, could ever have a chance of—of asking you to be his wife. That would be a different thing altogether."

"Ah, yes, if I were not lame! If I could ride, and row, and—and sail a boat!" said Freda with a quavering voice.

"No, no, just as you are, the sweetest, the dearest little——"

He stopped short, got up abruptly, and rushed at the fire, which he poked so vigorously that it went out. Then, quite subdued, he turned again to Freda, and holding his hands behind him, as he stood in a defiant attitude with his back to the fireplace, he asked abruptly:

"Would you like to know what I've been making up my mind to do, during these days that I've been living here like a rat in a hole?"

"Ye-es," said Freda without looking up.

"Well, you'll be shocked. At least, perhaps you won't be, but anybody else would be. I'm going to turn farm-labourer, and here, in the very neighbourhood where I was brought up a gentleman, as they call it."

The girl raised her head quickly, and looked him straight in the face, with shining, straightforward eyes.

"I think it is very brave of you," she said in a high, clear voice.

"Hundreds of well educated young fellows," he went on, flushed by her encouragement, "go out to Manitoba, and Texas, and those places, and do that or anything to keep themselves, and nobody thinks the less of them. Why shouldn't I do the same here, in my own country, where I know something about the way of farming, which will all come in by-and-by? You see, I know my family's disgraced, through my—my unfortunate cousin's escapade; for even if it's brought in manslaughter in a quarrel, as some of them say, he'll get penal servitude. But, disgrace or no disgrace, I can't bring myself to leave the old haunts; and as I've no money to farm this place, I'll get work either here, if it lets, or somewhere near, if it doesn't. I've made up my mind."

The obstinate look which Freda had seen on his face before came out more strongly than ever as he said these words. During the pause that followed, they heard voices and footsteps approaching, and then Captain Mulgrave opened the door. The breaking up of the organisation he had worked so long seemed already to have had a good moral effect on him, for he spoke cheerfully as he turned to John Thurley, who followed him.

"Here's the hermit! but oh, who's this in the anchorite's cell with him? Why, it's the nun!"

John Thurley looked deeply annoyed. He had an Englishman's natural feeling that he was very much the superior of a man who looked underfed; and it was this haggard-faced young fellow who, as he rightly guessed, had been the chief cause of the failure of his own suit. Captain Mulgrave's good-humored amusement over the discovery of the young people together woke in him, therefore, no responsive feeling. Before they were well in the room, Freda had slipped out of it, through the door by the fireplace, and was making her way up to the outer wall. Dick was at first inclined to be annoyed at the interruption; but when Captain Mulgrave explained the object of his visit and that of his companion, the young man's joy at the project they came to suggest was unbounded. This was the setting up of himself to farm the land, for the benefit of his aunt, to whom it had been left for life.

"Mr. Thurley is a connection of hers and wishes to see some provision made for her. So, as I felt sure you would be glad to do your best for her too," continued Captain Mulgrave, "and as you have some knowledge of farming, I suggested setting you up in a small way as farmer here, and extending operations if you proved successful. How would that meet your views?"

Dick was overwhelmed; he could scarcely answer coherently.

"I never expected such happiness, sir," he stammered, in a low voice. "I would rather follow the plough on this farm than be a millionaire, anywhere else. Why," he went on after a moment's pause, in a tone of eager delight, "I might—marry!"

He flushed crimson as Captain Mulgrave began to laugh.

"Well," said the latter, "I don't know that you could do better. You were always a good lad at heart, and my quarrel was never with you, but with your cousin. He used your services for his own advantage, but I must do you the justice to say it was never for yours. So find a wife if you can; I think you're the sort to treat a woman well."

Dick took the suggestion literally, and acted upon it at once. Leaving the two other men together in the darkening room, with some sort of excuse about seeing after the house, he went outside into the court-yard, and soon spied out Freda on the ruined outer wall. He was beside her in a few moments, looking down at her with a radiant face.

"I'm going to stay here—on the farm—to manage it myself—to be master here."

"Oh, Dick!" was all the girl could say, in a breathless way.

"It sounds too good for belief, doesn't it? But it's true. That old Thurley must be a good fellow, for he's going to help to start me. It's for my aunt's benefit he's doing it; he's a connection of hers."

"Oh, Dick, if you had had a fairy's wish, you couldn't have chosen more, could you?"

There was a pause before Dick answered, and during that pause he began to get nervous. At last he said:

"There is one more thing. Your father said——"

A pause.

"Well, what did my father say?"

"He said—I might marry. Is—it true?"

And it took Dick very few minutes to find out that it was.

THE END.

161

Florence Warden was the pseudonym of Florence Alice (Price) James.

Minor spelling inconsistencies (*e.g.* back-door/back door, farmhouse/farm-house, etc.) have been preserved.

Alterations to the text:

Add TOC.

Punctuation fixes: sentences missing periods, quotation mark pairings, etc.

[Chapter XIII]

Change "in which the jury had *veiwed* her father's body" to *viewed*.

[Chapter XXXI]

"and the other asked the way to *Oldastle* Farm." to *Oldcastle*.

"a good suggestion; and Dick took advantage *af* it." to *of*.

[End of text]